# GARDEN GAZEBO GALIVANT

# GARDEN GAZEBO GALLIVANT

# Book V

### Abby L. Vandiver

Find me on my website: www.abbyvandiver.com
Follow me on Twitter: @AbbyVandiver
Facebook: www.facebook.com/authorabbyl.vandiver

Cover Design by Shondra C. Longino

ISBN-13: 9781521299517

First Printing May 2017
Printed in the United States

10  9  8  7  6  5  4  3  2  1

# Dedication

*To my granddaughter, September, the wise one.*

Prologue

*Something old, something new, something borrowed, something blue . . .*

Old sayings sometimes get a bad rap. Being in use for hundreds of years, they started as an easy and memorable guide for life. But the smarter we got, the sooner those old adages began to be regarded as unscientific or incorrect, even downright silly. And being pinned superstition, or equally as condemning "old wives tales," certainly didn't help advocating for anyone to take heed.

And sure, you won't get stomach cramps if you go swimming less than an hour after eating, or get a windfall of money if the palm of your right hand itches. But c'mon, there must be something to them if they've hung around for generations and generations.

So, if we're honest, we all should be able to agree that there are sayings that do have some truth to them. Like "an apple a day, keeps the doctor away", or "honey calms a cough."

And some saying have been modernized, and now openly adhered to by millions, for example:

"Association brings on assimilation," is now all the rage under the law of attraction's maxim "like attracts like." Thousands follow the saw, and proclaim by just putting **good** vibes out in the air, good things will come your way.

But what about the old sayings about love? "Absence makes the heart grow fonder." "You can't buy love." "You can't find love, it will find you."

They too were made to help lovers heal broken hearts, endure love's entanglements, and to guide them through what every soul longs for. And as of late, I've begun to believe that there's something to them. I'm beginning to see that love makes the heart and person strong. Strong enough to make it through anything.

It was Maya Angelou that said "Love recognizes no barriers. It jumps hurdles, leaps fences, penetrates walls to arrive at its destination full of hope.

I think that that's true, even when the road to that destination is paved in murder . . .

Chapter One
Thursday, 6am

*Three days before the wedding . . .*

It sounded like a dog wailing compilation.

It was sunrise, a pinkish sky still hung over the horizon. The air was crisp and filled with the smell of magnolia from the abundance of trees dotting the greens of the town square that sprouted the flower. I'd taken Cat, Miss Vivee's wheaten Scottish terrier, and we'd walked to the center of town.

I pulled out my cell to check the time, and noticed the reminder I'd set. I smiled. It was only three days until the big day.

I'd thrown on a pair of sweat pants, a T-shirt and grabbed my dark blue windbreaker jacket to endure the morning chill. Short on time, I still just had to see the progress on the wedding gazebo. After a quick "looksee" as Miss Vivee would say, I'd go back to the Maypop, eat and shower before going to the airport in Augusta. My mother and brother were flying in for the big celebration.

I just couldn't get enough of visiting the spot where the ceremony would take place. A garden gazebo wedding.

*What could be more beautiful?*

I walked toward it wanting to see the flowering plants Miss Vivee had directed be put around the gazebo, and the tree we'd planted to commemorate the marriage. I was so excited to see how it was being transformed.

Well I had been . . .

Until the wailing started.

Cat, head tilted, ears perked, tail wagging on high, looked up at me and I looked at her.

"What's going on, girl? Who's doing all that barking?"

She let out a bark of her own and took off running.

"I didn't mean for you to go and see," I yelled after her. "Cat! Come back here,"

But I don't think she could hear me over the yelping of the other dogs.

*What the hey . . .*

"Cat! C'mere, girl," I yelled out and started chasing after her. But I didn't get far. I hadn't even gone twenty-five feet when a pack of dogs (okay maybe not a pack, but more than I cared to see) rounded a corner and came romping my way.

They sprang from the other side of the street, around a slow moving (thank goodness) black car with tinted windows up onto the square greens, and across the grass toward me.

Crap!

I did a U-turn, head in the air, arms pumping, I zigged-zagged across the town square trying to get away from them, but it didn't take long for them to overtake me. Trying to hop out of their way, the blue, nylon leash of a Saint Bernard loping past wrapped around my ankle, knocked me over, and dragged me a foot or two before the restraint unraveled from my leg. My cell phone went up in the air, and one of those canine creatures loping past, leapt and caught it like a Gold Medal Olympian Frisbee Flying Champ, and was back in the pack without missing a beat.

*Crap!*

I glanced down to make sure my engagement ring hadn't slipped off my finger in the commotion. My chunk of gems was still new, and I felt for it often. I hadn't gotten used to it yet. I sighed in relief, the sun refracted off of it and the sparkled created winked at me letting me know it was still there.

"Stop! Stop!" I heard a female voice coming toward me. "Please stop!" it squealed.

I rolled over on my belly and watched a twenty-something, dark haired, baggy jean-wearing, and from the way her arms were flailing, clearly frustrated girl running toward me. "Are you okay?" she asked hurrying over to me. "I don't know what happened. They just kind of got away from me." She reached down, anchored her foot into the grass, and pulled me up by my arm.

"They *did* get away from you," I said correcting any doubt she had about what happened. Upon standing, I brushed the dirt off, and turned to see the dogs run back across the street from where they originally hailed.

"Why do you have so many dogs?" I said and turned back to her.

"It's my job," she said almost indignantly. "I'm the dog walker."

*Not a very good one.*

"My pho-" But before I could finish my sentence, she took off.

"I have to go," she said running. "I have to catch the dogs."

"They have my phone!" I yelled after her. "And my dog."

She turned to face me and hunched her shoulders.

*What did that mean? Are they just lost forever?*

I watched her until she disappeared around a small watershed at the far corner of the square. Then I just stood there, unsure of what to do next – until I heard the dogs. Again. Then I saw them. They were coming my way. Springing from behind a bush at full throttle, they must've circled around.

*Crap!*

I took off zigzagging across the lawn. (I don't know why because that strategy hadn't worked for me the first time.) I turned to see them gaining on me, Cat leading the pack. I crisscrossed through the small grove of magnolia trees, headed in the direction of the gazebo, and dived over a bank of bushes. Once I hit the ground, I tucked and rolled landing underneath the gazebo. Out of sight and out of breath. I sucked in gulps of air and tried to keep as quiet as I could so as not to give away my position. I figured I'd just wait them out. Inept Dog Walker Girl would have to get control of them at some point.

Then I thought about Miss Vivee's dog. She would kill me if anything happened to Cat.

"Ugh!" I grunted. "I have to go and get that dog."

I crawled out of my hiding place, stood up and raked the dirt of my hands and backside. Then I listened for the thundering herd of paws, and headed in that direction. Picking up my pace with every thought of Cat taking to the road with the pack, never to be seen again, or worse, coming to a tragic end in a fight with a vicious pit bull. I was nearly at a full trot when my trek came to a sudden, screeching halt. There under a large magnolia tree, right behind the wedding gazebo – face up, one arm splayed – was a dead body.

*Crap!*

## Chapter Two

It was a girl. Young. She looked the same age as that dubious dog walker. She was dressed in a bright yellow jogging suit, the jacket zipped up to her neck. She had a long ponytail that was now sprawled out from her head with a yellow ribbon tied around it. Her right hand holding her left arm.

I absently reached for my phone inside my jacket pocket to call the Sheriff. I wrapped my fingers around it, and yanking it from my overstuffed jacket pocket, a crumpled brown bag fell to the ground, almost on top of Dead Girl.

*Geesh! I'ma mess up the crime scene . . .*

I looked at my hand, I was holding my wallet. *Oh crap!* I'd forgotten. I'd lost my phone to the dogs. I bent down to pick up the bag I'd dropped and a bee came buzzing by. I swerved out of its way, and dropped my wallet.

*Oh goodness.*

I managed to pick up both the paper bag and my wallet without touching Dead Girl and secured both back inside my pocket. I stepped over Dead Girl and plopped down on the black and white wrought iron bench that sat next to her and let out a loud sigh.

I looked down at the body. Her mouth opened, eyes wide, it was like death had been a painful, unexpected surprise.

I nudged her with the toe of my tennis shoe. Nothing.

*Darn that Miss Vivee and her destiny divinations. I just can't deal with anymore dead people.*

This just couldn't be happening. Not today. Not right before the wedding. And I could tell from her face, and age, that it probably wasn't death by natural cause. It was murder.

I glanced over at the gazebo - now a crime scene – and covered my face with my hands.

"Aaahhhhhh!" Came a scream from behind. It startled me. I jumped, nearly falling from my seat, I caught myself and hopped up. I spun around and saw the dog walker standing at the edge of the bench. She had rounded up the dogs, and somehow got them to stick with her. Then I spied my nearly new, iPhone6 in the mouth of that same St. Bernard that had bowled me over.

Dog Walker Girl covered her mouth with one hand, her eyes as big as Dead Girl's. "No! No! No!" was her muffled wail. And the dogs echoed her every cry. From scratchy throated howls, to high pitched yowls, they were her back-up chorus. Still whimpering, she backed away and stumbled over one of them.

"Watch out!" I tried to reach forward, over the bench, to catch her from tripping, I was too far away and she spilled over and fell to the ground.

The yowls turned into wails.

*Oh my gosh! They're going to wake up the whole town.*

I rounded the bench, and it was my turn to help her up. "Are you okay?" I said.

She nodded. "Yeah. I am." She sniffed and glanced at Dead Girl. "Is she alright?" she asked me.

"Nooo," I shook my head. "I don't think so."

"Oh!" she moaned and dropped to her knees.

I didn't know what to say. She seemed pretty upset, and having a hard time staying on her feet. "Did you know her?" I asked and reached down to help her up. Again. This time I walked her to the bench and sat her down.

"Yes," she said as if it should be obvious to me. "That's Kimmie."

"Okaaay. Well we need to get someone over here to help Kimmie."

She stared at the body and then up at me. "Get her to a hospital?" She started nodding vigorously. "Yeah, that's a good idea" She swallowed hard and sniffed back her tears. "Can you call 911?"

I glanced over at my phone. It was full of dog saliva. "Yeah," I said. "We can call for help. I can call the Sheriff-"

"And an ambulance," she said interrupting me. She swiped her hand across her eyes. "Tell them to hurry."

No need for an ambulance, I wanted to say. She didn't seem like she comprehended that "Kimmie" was gone and I didn't want to be the one to say it out loud.

"I need to use your phone," I said and stuck out my hand. "I don't think mine is operable." I nodded my head toward the wet, sticky Apple glob that Mr. St. Bernard held on to.

"I don't have a phone!" She was nearly yelling, the realization hitting her like a brick. "Oh, my God, no!" She started shaking her head. "Oh, it was Kimmie!" She looked up at me.

"What was Kimmie?"

"The dogs don't like my ringtone. I was going to change it, but Kimmie-" she looked at the body. "Kimmie knew how much I liked it and she told me don't change it, just leave my phone at home. 'What could happen?' she had told me."

"It's okay," I said. I didn't know if I should pat her, or hug her. "Sheriff's office is right across the square-"

"You can't leave Kimmie!"

"I have to," I said. "I have to get help." I looked at the body and back up at her. "What's your name?"

"Seppie."

"Seppie?" I asked.

She sniffed and nodded. "Short for September."

1

"Okay, September. I'm Logan." I pointed to myself. "You stay here with Kimmie." I pointed to Dead Girl. "I'll go get help."

"You go get help," she said between sobs.

"You can stay here," I said.

"I'll stay here," she repeated. The sobs were getting louder.

"And don't touch the body."

"*Aaahh, haahhh,*" she started wailing. "I won't touch the body."

*Okay, maybe I shouldn't have mentioned "the body."*

"I'll be back as soon as I can," I said.

She nodded. "What about the dogs?" she shouted at me, as if she wasn't two feet away. She took the bottom of her shirt and wiped her tear stained face.

"You keep the dogs," I said in a normal voice, wanting to keep us calm. "Except for Cat, I'm taking her with me." I took off trotting. "C'mon Cat." She barked and came running. "And try to keep them under control," I shouted to September over my shoulder.

*I don't think it's her ringtone that upsets those dogs,* I thought as I jogged across the square to the sheriff's office. She is just a bad dog walker.

*And poor Kimmie . . .*

"Oh crap!" I said. I'd realized that as soon as Miss Vivee got a whiff of a murder she'd want to try and solve it, wedding be damned. She'd have me pick up her notebook from Hadley's, her No. 2 pencils, and we be off on a suspect hunt quicker than a cat could lick its behind. Special day, or no special day. And of course, she'd want to drag Mac along.

*Why is this happening to me?*

I counted up the dead bodies and I sprinted along.

One, Gemma Burke. Two, Oliver Gibson. I numbered them on my fingers. Three, Aaron Coulter. Four, Laura Tyler. Five, Jack Wagner. And I can't forget Jairo Zacapa. *Shoot. I need another hand to count.* Jairo is number six, well actually he was *numero uno.* He was the first dead body I'd seen that hadn't been two thousand years old.

And now Kimmie.

*Number seven.*

I slowed down, out of breath from going faster than my usual turtle's pace. Trying to even out my breathing I knew that this was going to take all of the joy out of my day.

*How did my life go so wrong?* I thought as I walked the last few feet to the police station. Archaeologist turned amateur sleuth? This couldn't be what was meant to be for me to do.

My mother would have a cardiac arrest if she knew.

I was the only one of her three children to follow in her footsteps and now I'd taken a really bad detour.

*My mother!* Crap. I had to go and pick her up at the airport. I reached in my pocket for my phone to check the time, but of course it wasn't there. "Oh. Man." I thought about that phone chomping dog. I

1

was sure, by now, the inside of my cell phone had been fried. No bowl of rice could ever dry that thing out.

I reached the sheriff's office, picked up Cat, putting her in my arm, I turned the knob to the door. A tinkle from the little bell over the door announced my arrival.

"Who's dead now?" Sheriff Lloyd Haynes glanced up at me. He said it as soon as I walked through the door.

*How could he know?*

I dropped Cat out of my arms and looked down at myself to make sure I hadn't somehow magically obtained a sign that read, "I Found a Dead Girl at the Gazebo" then turned around and looked behind me to make sure September hadn't followed me carrying one.

"How'dya know?" I asked.

"That's the only time I see you, Logan," he said.

I scrunched up my nose. Not a good impression of anyone to have of me.

"So?" he said. "What you got?"

"It's Kimmie," I said.

"That's who's dead?"

I nodded. He looked at me for a moment, over at his dispatcher, and then back at me. "Kimmie Hunt?"

"I'm not sure of her last name," I said.

"How do you know her name?" he asked as he walked over to the coat rack. He plucked his four-dented hat from the knob and placed it on his head.

"Seppie . . . Uhm, September told me."

"Seppie Love?"

I held up my hands. "I don't know her last name either."

"Call the Coroner, Mae Lynn," he said to the dispatcher. "And no one else," he seemed to emphasize. "I don't want no onlookers until I can get her identified and remove the body from the scene . . ." he looked at me up and down spotting the dirt all over me. "Where is she?" he asked.

Feeling self-conscious, I dusted off my clothes, swiped my hands together and tried to smooth down my hair. "Over behind the gazebo," I said and pointed a finger over my shoulder.

"Ain't ya'll decorating for the wedding over there?" he asked.

I took in a breath, and let out a long, deep sigh. "Yes," I said. "That's where the wedding is. In three days."

He chuckled. "You've got my apologies, but you know I'm gonna have to close that place down. At least 'til we get this thing figured out."

"Yeah," I mumbled, feeling agitated.

"Is Bay in yet?"

*Oh no*, I thought, and felt like I was going to cry. It really hit me that if Bay got involved with this murder, and the gazebo got shut down, there was no way a wedding was going to take place anytime soon. I squinted my eyes to keep the tears from coming.

1

"Logan," the Sheriff said my name. "I asked you if Bay got in town yet."

I closed my eyes and shook my head. "I don't know," I said, my voice shaky. I opened my eyes and looked at him. "He's supposed to get here today, sometime." I looked at the Sheriff and hunched my shoulders. "I don't know."

"Well. I'm going by and pick up Junior Appletree from the library," Sheriff Haynes said. "He's my voluntary, temporary deputy." He walked over to the door and held it open for me. "I know I'ma need some help. So when Bay gets in, can you let him know?"

"That's not Bay's jurisdiction over there," I said practically pouting. "And with the wedding and everything, he's not going to be able to help."

"But that's the way it goes," he said.

"The way what goes?" I asked.

"A dead body shows up, you and Miss Vivee put on your sleuthing hats, and somehow, for some reason, it always ends up being Bay's jurisdiction."

"Oh. So it's like a script?" I frowned up my face thinking about Miss Vivee's pronouncement that it was my destiny to help her solve murders. "That's how you know someone's dead because I show up? And that's how you know Bay's going to be involved? Because that's the way it always happens?"

"Yep," he said. "Since you got here, murder in Yasamee always unfolds the same way – just like a story in a book."

I let out a snort.

"Or, I can give him a call," he said and walked toward the door. A small grin crept across his face. "If'n you not inclined to." I opened my mouth to speak, but he cut me off. "And before you get your britches in a knot, I'm gonna need you to meet us back over there. I gotta take your statement."

I glanced up at the clock on the wall. "Okay. I can do that, Sheriff. But I need to pick up my mother and brother from the airport. I'm running late now." I looked down at myself. There was no way I was going to be able to give my statement, get a shower, change and get out to the airport on time.

"We'll get through it as quickly as possible," he said. "I'll see you over there in five minutes."

*Ugh!* I thought. This was not turning out to be a good day.

Then I thought maybe I shouldn't complain. My day was definitely going better than Kimmie's.

1

Chapter Three

I decided to stop at Jellybean's Café and pick up a cup of coffee before heading back to the gazebo. I needed the caffeine. With the way things were going, and not looking forward to being late picking my mother and brother, I could use any help I could get.

I turned the opposite way that the Sheriff had gone, Cat following at my heels. I started to cut across the street and walk diagonally to Jellybean's across the square when I noticed that same black car I'd seen earlier. It was still moving at that snail's pace, but this time there were no dogs getting in its way. I turned around and went back to the sidewalk. Over my shoulder and out the corner of my eye I watched as it crawled down the street. Ready to go back to the Sheriff's office if the situation became more ominous, it suddenly picked up its speed and drove past me. It turned down one of the streets off the square and disappeared.

I blew out a breath. *Who is that?*

I decided to walk to the corner and go around the square. Sticking closer to the storefronts. I felt safer.

Cat noticed Mac before I did, and ran up to him. He was sitting on a bench along the side of the street, hands folded, hat pulled down on head, looking solemn.

"Hey, Mac," I said. I tried to sound cheery.

He smiled at me. "What's your story, morning glory?" he said and tipped his hat.

I chuckled. "Nothing." I sat down next to him. "Did you see that black car? The one with the tinted windows?"

"No. Something wrong?"

I shook the notion of fear out of my head. "No. It's okay," I said and looked at him. "What are you doing here?"

"Waiting on the florist to open," he said reaching down to scratch Cat behind her ears.

I turned around and looked at the dark, locked tight florist shop. I noticed the hours of operation painted on the door. "It's only about seven," I said remembering the time on the Sheriff's clock. "The florist won't be open for another two hours.

"I can wait."

"Two hours?"

"At my age, I don't have anything but time."

"Couldn't find anything better to do with your time?" I asked. "What about coming over and having breakfast at the Maypop?" Cat let out a bark when I mentioned her home. I picked her up and put her on my lap.

1

"I don't want to get caught up in all the flurry of the wedding preparations. And I wanted to order a boutonnière."

"Boutonnière?" I turned to look again at the florist shop, then at Mac. "You know you do have one ordered, right? Miss Vivee made sure to get you one. A special one."

"I want to get my own," he said showing a little more independence than he usually did when it came to Miss Vivee.

I looked at him out of the side of my eye. He didn't seem his usual, chipper self.

"What are you doing here?" he asked before I could question him about his demeanor. "You're out pretty early"

"Found a dead body."

"They're really starting to pile up, aren't they?"

"You know Miss Vivee said it's my – well *our* – shared destiny."

"So, I've heard."

"Looks like you're in our destiny, too, Mac. Haven't solved one without your help."

I saw a glimmer of a smile.

"So what happened?" he asked.

"When?"

"With the dead body," he said.

"Oh. Yeah. I went to check on the Gazebo-"

"This early?"

"Yeah." I chuckled. "I wanted to see how it looked." I said and he smiled. "To be honest, I go there a couple of times a day."

"You're excited, huh?"

I smiled back. "Yes. I really am. Anyway," I patted his hand. "I just wanted to see it before I left to go and pick up my mother and Micah from the airport."

"And was everything okay?"

"You mean other than the dead body?"

"Yes. Other than that," he nodded his head.

"There's a table in the middle of the gazebo that isn't supposed to be there. It wasn't there last night when I visited."

"You women make such a fuss over these things." He laughed. "How often do you go up there?"

"I told you I go a lot." I chuckled. "Anyway, it's an easy fix. To move the table," I said. "I'll talk to Marge, the wedding planner." I nodded my head slowly suddenly thinking that with a dead body lying across the street, right behind the gazebo, the joyous occasion around the corner for us might not be an appropriate topic of conversation. "Easy fix." I said again but not with as much enthusiasm.

"Easier fix than the problem the dead body poses, huh?" It's like he had read my thoughts.

"Much." I sighed. "So you want to walk over there with me? I have to go back and meet the Sheriff."

"Who's there with the body now? Not good to leave it unattended."

"There was a dog walker out this morning. She was very upset about it. Hysterical, really."

"Ahh, Seppie Love. Yasamee's eminent dog walker."

"'Eminent' is not the word I'd use for her," I said. "And yeah, due to her dog walking skills my phone got filled with saliva-"

"Saliva?" he interrupted and stuck out is tongue as if he was trying to get rid of a bad taste.

"Ha! That's a story all on its own, Mac." I swiped my hands through the air. "Anyway. Seppie left her phone at home. So one of us had to go and get the Sheriff."

He stood up. "I'll walk with you and you can tell me about the body," he said.

"Nothing much to tell," I said taking his arm and helping him up. I handed him his cane that he had leaned against the bench. "She was lying behind the gazebo, right next to a bench, underneath the magnolia trees."

"What did she die from?" he asked.

"I don't know," I said and hunched my shoulders. "I can't look at people the way you and Miss Vivee do and know the cause of death."

"Well, when you get as old as the two of us," Mac said. "You'll know a lot of things. Sometimes though, that knowledge isn't very helpful because you're too old to use it." He smiled, but it looked strained.

I looped my arm around his, and helped him step off the curb. We walked in silence back over to the gazebo, and by the time we got there, the sheriff still hadn't arrived.

"What took you so long?" September asked as we approached. She stood up and came over to us. "This place is full of bees, they were making the dogs go crazy."

*I don't think it's the bees . . .*

"I thought you were getting the sheriff." She said and looked at Mac.

"I did get the Sheriff," I said. "He's on his way." I pointed to Mac with my thumb. "This is Dr. Whitson."

"I know who he is," September said. "Can he help her?"

Mac walked over to the body, bent down and touched her face. Then he felt her neck. He took his fingers and closed her eyes. Standing up, he looked at September. "No one can help her," Mac said. He took off his jacket and spread it over her face. "She's gone."

"Dead!" September said as if she'd never thought about the possibility.

"Yes," he said. "Dead."

Her knees buckled, and she went down. Again. This time I just left her there. Figured that was the best place for her.

"What do you think, Mac?" I asked once he took a look at it.

"Not sure," he said.

2

"Not sure?" I almost couldn't believe those words came out of his mouth. "You're not sure of what?"

He looked at me, his eyes looking blank. "I think I should go and get Vivee," he said. "I hadn't wanted to see her today, but I guess it's for the best."

"Oh really?" That didn't sound anything like the usual I-adore-Vivienne-Pennywell Mac that I knew. "You don't want to see her? What's gotten in to you today, Mac?" I asked.

"Same thing that gets in me every day – a little coffee, a slice of toast, and a handful of pills."

Chapter Four

We had to talk Seppie into staying there alone (well with the dogs) until the sheriff could get there. I knew I'd told him I'd wait, but that plane wasn't going to. It would land and drop my mother off whether I was there or not, and I couldn't just have her and my brother, Micah, standing around.

Mac wanted to go get Miss Vivee.

"She's still sleeping," I said.

"Probably not sleeping," Mac said. "She's an early riser."

"Well sleep or not, I just don't know if it's a good idea to get her involved" I said. "With the wedding and all, she'll get distracted."

"Don't you worry none about that," Mac said. "She'll be fine for the wedding, and she'll find out soon enough on her own about Kimmie."

We chatted all the way back, and I never let on that I'd worried that maybe Mac couldn't walk as far as the Maypop, the bed and breakfast owned by Miss Vivee and her daughters, Renmar and Brie. I didn't want to say anything, and by the time we walked up

2

the brick walkway to the large colonial, I was glad I hadn't. He and his cane were amazing.

Mac went off to find Miss Vivee, he figured she was in her greenhouse. I headed upstairs to my room. Once there, I studied my reflection in the cheval mirror. Grass stains, dirt, and dog saliva covered me. Running out of time or not, I knew I couldn't go looking like I looked.

I went into the ensuite bathroom, washed my face and hands, threw on a clean pair of khaki-colored shorts, and slipped a gray tank top over my head. Sheriff Haynes couldn't get anything else worthwhile from me. If helping Miss Vivee was my destiny, my part didn't come into play until after the cause of death was ascertained, and that would take her expertise. Mac would make sure she got there, I was going to pick up my mother.

Chapter Five

It hadn't been that long since I'd seen my mother, but I was excited about her coming to Georgia. I hopped on the highway, turned up the music and started singing along with Robin Thicke's *Morning Sun* and thought about Bay.

Bay and I had taken that trip to Cleveland, at my parents' request, to get engaged. He hadn't wanted to ask for my hand in marriage without my father's blessing, – southern gentleman that he was – and after calling him to get it, my parents suggested that Bay and I come for a visit, give me my ring there, and he could meet my family – kill two birds with one stone.

*And oh, what a ring it is!* I glanced down at it, my ring finger, now heavier by at least two carats. I turned my hand from side to side to admire it, the bling almost blinding me.

I exhaled. *Boy, I can't wait for my wedding day.*

Once Bay and I got to Cleveland, my parents really took to him, and so did my uncles, all five of them. They acted if he'd always been a part of the family. My mother's baby sister, Claire, was so

2

enamored with him that she insisted we stay at her house. She lived in a big, six bedroom house where my uncles usually camped out, but she gave them all the boot to accommodate us. She even threw us a big, impromptu engagement party. But with all the commotion I hadn't really had time to sit down and talk to my mother. I knew there was a lot she wanted to say to me.

I drove up to the curb near the baggage claim of United Airlines, and she was the first person I saw. Justin Dickerson. Famous, or in some circles infamous, Biblical archaeologist and my mother. And juggling the luggage was my big brother Micah. My father was driving a U-Haul down with my belongings, so they decided that Micah would fly down with her, keep her company and keep her safe – something he and my father did after she had a few too many Indiana Jones-like encounters with would-be killers.

Sheriff Haynes thought me and Miss Vivee's antics unfolded like a book, he'd be on the edge of his seat if he'd read a book about the things my mother had done in her work. It was one of the reasons I'd become an archaeologists. My work had never been as exciting as hers though.

Well until now.

Only my excitement had nothing to do with my work.

My mother had discovered an alternative history to man's beginnings, and her travels had taken her all around the world.

Mine took me to Georgia.

And now it was official, I was making Georgia my home. At least for now.

My mother had had a full life and it had made her strong. Justin Dickerson had been given a boy's name by her mother, and then did the same with her two girls. Me – Logan, and my older sister, Courtney. She had excavated in the Holy Land, Egypt, and Turkey. She spoke seven languages, and had an eidetic memory. Anything she read was permanently seared into her brain.

I hadn't inherited any of those abilities from my mother, but my naturally curly hair was definitely in the twenty-three chromosomes she'd contributed to my DNA. But that was it. She was dark-skin, where my light skin had been passed down to me from my father. She was short at 5'4"and round compared to my 5'8" slender frame, and with her in her late fifties, she had slowed down considerably in her work, now only teaching a class or two at Case Western Reserve, a top ranked research university in Cleveland, never liking to play in the dirt as much as I did.

But I supposed her biggest claim to fame was that she had discovered that man, just like us – same DNA as she liked to say – had originated on Mars.

But that's a whole different story.

2

I loved talking archaeology with my mother, and I knew I had made her proud being the only one of her three children that had chosen it as my profession.

I took in a deep breath before reaching for the car door handle. I didn't want to let on that I'd spent my morning at a crime scene.

I hadn't told my mother much about the dead bodies that were falling all around me. She'd been with me when I saw my first one. It scared the life (and pee) out of me. She had to yell at me to get me to calm down. But I didn't know how to tell her how they'd been racking up as of late, and how much more comfortable with them I'd become. I usually told her everything, but becoming an amateur sleuth, per my destiny as Miss Vivee put it, wasn't just something I felt one should share with their mother. Especially a mother who'd spent thousands of dollars on educating that child. And not in the field of forensics.

"I can't wait for you to meet Miss Vivee," I said, helping my mother into the car. It had become a habit with me now. I always got Miss Vivee in and buckled her seat belt. I had to catch myself from reaching for it before closing the door. Micah loaded their luggage in the trunk and got in the back seat.

At fifty-eight, overweight and busty, my mother liked to act older than she was. She was funny, and smart. Really smart. Most kids think their parents are smart when their young, but once they get out in the world, and learn a thing or two they begin to believe they're just as smart, if not smarter than their parents.

I, nor my siblings, would ever think that about my mother. The older we got, the smarter she seemed. She believed that learning was a life-long process, and she instilled that in us.

*I wonder how smart she'll think it is that I'm solving whodunits in small town Yasamee . . .*

I clicked on my blinkers, took the ramp that led to the highway back to Yasamee, then glanced over at my mother. I smiled. I had really missed my "Mommy."

Out the corner of my eye, I watched as she ran her hand through her hair. The edges of it grayer than I remembered from seeing her just a couple weeks earlier. Her hair was long, but thinning thanks to my grandmother's genes, and her dark skin was smooth and void of wrinkles. She looked much younger than she was, or acted.

"Miss Vivee sounds like a hoot," she said and smiled at me.

"She is. You'll like her."

"You know I have a soft spot for old people," she said.

I laughed. *I must have one too*, I thought. *Miss Vivee and Mac are my new best friends.*

"It's awfully hot down here," my mother said.

"It's the south," I said.

"It's been hot at home," Micah chimed in. "Ma, you know it's been like ninety degrees all summer."

3

"Summer's almost over," she said. "And snow'll be falling." She looked at me. "You won't see any of that, huh?"

I knew she meant that I wouldn't be home. She knew that marrying Bay meant that Cleveland would never be my home again. I could also hear her thoughts in between the words she did voice. I knew what she really wanted to say, was that I wouldn't be working, either. Which to me, didn't make any sense. If I were working, I still wouldn't be at home.

"I heard about a dig over in Fiji," I said.

"Fiji?" She turned and looked at me. "What in the world is there to dig there?"

"Everything isn't about Mars, Mommy."

"Oh, let's not talk about that," she said and waved her hand. "I need a break from worrying about if I'm doing the right thing in hiding our history." She turned and stared out of the window.

"You still worry about that?" I said.

"All the time," Micah said answering in her stead. "Should she tell? Shouldn't she tell?" I looked in the rearview mirror and saw him shaking his head. "Grammy told her she either needed to crap or get off the pot, only she didn't use the word 'crap.'"

I laughed. I missed my grandmother. She was as feisty as Miss Vivee, but she cussed like a sailor.

"Hopefully, the wedding will take my mind off of it," she said.

"You're the one that taught me – all of us," I looked back at my brother then over at my mother.

"That an archaeologist is the re-creator of history. And it's our job to tell the world about it. Maybe you should heed your own words and do just that. Share what you know."

"The world isn't ready to know what I know. Our true history," she said. "You know that's how I feel."

"What do you think is going to happen?" I asked. "If you tell history as it actually unfolded?"

"She thinks they'll come and drag her out of the house, torches blazing, pitch forks perched, and impale her head on a stake."

"Oh my," I said. I looked at my mother. "Is that what you think?"

"Nooo," she said and let her eyes drift away. "Not all the time. Sometimes I think they'll just put me a padded room. Head intact."

"Yeah, so let's talk about the wedding," I said.

We definitely needed to change the subject and take her mind off her crazy ruminations.

Chapter Six

"Stop the car." My mother insisted we stop as I drove past the square after entering Yasamee. There were still a handful of bystanders at the gazebo and evidently she wanted to know what that was about. "What's going on over there?"

I had circled through the historic district of Augusta, and driven her down the coastline so she could see the Savannah River. Perhaps she thought there was a tourist attraction on the greens of the square.

*If she only knew.*

"There's nothing to see there, Ma." I lifted my foot off the break ready to drive past.

"How do you know?" she said. "Stop the car."

I took in a breath and pressed back down on the brake. "A dead body was found there this morning."

"Oh my," she said. "I thought this was an idyllic little place. This is as bad as Cleveland."

I wanted to protest, but in the little time I'd been a resident in Yasamee, the crime rate had almost become comparable.

"I want to see," she said. "Park. Right there." She ordered and pointed.

I pulled over, parking illegally. I wasn't too worried about getting a ticket. I could see the sheriff from where we were.

And there, in the middle of it all, was Miss Vivee. She was dressed in her signature thin, cornflower blue coat with a round color. She had on tan-colored rubber rain boots with big orange dots on them. Her long gray braid hung over her shoulder.

As we neared the area, I could see that the body was still there. Someone had cordoned off the area and people had gathered around. September and her dogs were gone.

I pulled my mother in the direction of Miss Vivee.

"Where are you taking me?" she asked.

"I want you to meet someone."

"Hi," Miss Vivee said when we walked up. "Who you got here?"

"This is my mother, Justin Dickerson," I said. "And my brother, Micah."

Miss Vivee smiled a wide grin. "So nice to meet you, Dear," she said to my mother and linked her arm through hers. "So nice to meet *both* of you." She nodded at my brother. "I'm Vivienne Pennywell, but you can call me Vivee."

"Oh! You're Miss Vivee. It's so nice to meet you too," my mother said, a wide smile on her face. "We just fell in love with your grandson, and he and Logan told us so many good things about you."

3

"Don't you believe any of it," Miss Vivee said, leaning over and lowering her voice. "Probably nary a word is true." My mother laughed.

"Where's Mac," I asked.

"He went home," Miss Vivee said. "Might have to take him some tea. He seems out of sorts. I've got some St. John's Wort tea in my cabinet, it'll help him." She looked at my mother. "I'm a Voodoo herbalist, you know. I can cure practically any malady with my herb mixtures."

"Really?" My mother chuckled.

"Uhh!" Micah was ducking up and down and waving his hand.

"What's wrong?" I asked.

"It's a bee!" He jumped and turned around trying to get out of its way.

"You scared of a bee?" I said. "Don't be such a girl!"

"I'm not a girl," he said. "You ever been stung by one? Those things hurt."

"A few of them have been out," Miss Vivee said. "I think maybe it's the potted plants I had placed here. I'll have Marge change them out."

"So what's going on?" my mother said and pointed to Kimmie.

"Logan didn't tell you?" Miss Vivee looked at me out the corner of her eye. "Your daughter found her this morning. Dead as a doornail."

"Before you came to pick us up?" My mother looked at me.

"Yep," I said feeling a little uneasiness with my one word answer.

"Well why wouldn't you tell me that?" My mother said and looked around. "And isn't this the gazebo where the wedding is going to take place?"

I nodded.

She looked at me then at Miss Vivee. "Well that couldn't be good."

"Not to worry," Miss Vivee said. "Logan and I will have this figured out before the wedding with time to spare."

"You and Logan?" My mother asked and looked at me. "Have it figured out? What does that mean, Logan?"

I lowered my eyes. I didn't want to answer that question. I let my eyes drift over to Kimmie. Mac's jacket had been removed from her face, and someone had taken off her yellow jogging jacket.

"Oh!" my mother said, apparently having followed my eyes. It took her only a minute to notice something I hadn't. She glanced at me then over at Miss Vivee. "Those holes in her arm. It couldn't be . . ." She shook her head.

"Yes?" Miss Vivee said, cocking her head to the side, I could see a glimmer of excitement in her eyes. "You know what that is?"

"I know how she died," my mother said. "If that's what you mean."

I perked up, paying attention. *She couldn't know.*

"Do tell," Miss Vivee said.

3

"Has the coroner said anything yet?" she asked Miss Vivee.

"Seems like he's on a fishing trip. Left before daybreak. That's why she's still lying here. Mac gave her a once over as a preliminary. Sheriff's trying to find an ambulance or truck to cart her out."

"Cart her out?" My mother chuckled.

"Maybe we could use that truck of yours," Miss Vivee said to me.

"I don't think so," I said.

"Don't be rude," my mother said. "If they need your help, you should give it."

If she only knew how much stuff Miss Vivee dragged me into, she wouldn't be offering any of my help to anyone around here.

"So what killed her?" I said directing my question to my mother. I was pretty sure Miss Vivee had already figured it out.

They looked at each other and back at me. "An Asian Hornet," they said in unison.

Miss Vivee smiled at my mother, and then at me. "How come you never had your mother come here before?" she said evidently quite pleased with her. "Come with me, Justin," Miss Vivee said to her. "Let's see if Sheriff Haynes needs our help with anything else." She practically pushed my mother around the yellow taped area.

I let my eyes follow them around the body and they landed on Junior Appletree.

*Sheriff Haynes might just need their help,* I thought.

Junior had been the janitor at the library for nearly thirty years. But it seemed that experience hadn't given him any skills for solving crime. He didn't seem to know what to do. He followed behind the sheriff and then stumbled over his own feet trying to get out of the sheriff's way. Good thing Junior was temporary, he was just as bumbling as the last deputy.

That made me think about the old deputy – Colin Pritchard. I laughed to myself. To think I had a crush on him when I first arrived, and then he turned out to be Gemma Burke's murderer. I sure could pick 'em.

*But I did do a good job picking Bay.* That thought put a smile on my face.

Oh! Wait! Maybe now that I knew my destiny was solving crimes, perhaps my feelings for Colin Pritchard were just that I had honed in on him because deep down somewhere – really deep down – I had a sixth sense about him.

I had thought that with all the murders happening that I must be a murder magnet, but what if I was a "murderer" magnet? Like Miss Vivee and Mac could spot the cause of death, maybe I could spot the killer . . .

I had zoomed in on Colin. I thought it was feelings of like (or lust) but maybe it was a vibe – a "killer" vibe that I was starting to develop.

3

And I hadn't liked that Tom Bowlen either, Oliver's killer . . . *Wait*. Maybe that was Miss Vivee that hadn't like him. *Okay . . .*

I tried to think about all the murders I'd been involved with, then I pictured each killer in my mind. The last murderer, Marigold Kent, had been on my radar. Okay, so it wasn't that I picked her as the culprit, but I knew she was a liar.

That's something, right?

*If it is my destiny to solve murders,* I thought. *It's logical that I might have a special "power," too.*

Okay, if I were honest, I'd have to admit that I hadn't had any "feelings" about all the other killers.

So maybe I just hadn't picked up anything because I hadn't completely developed my super sleuthing skill of detecting the murderer yet.

*Makes sense, right?*

Perhaps it had been sparked with Colin and I just needed to work on it. Build it up. Practice it.

I nodded. Straightening my shoulders, I wiggled my fingers, cleared my mind and blew out a breath.

I scanned the crowd that had gathered. Miss Vivee had said that a killer always returned to the crime scene.

*Perhaps he (or she) was here right now.*

Wait . . . I tilted my head. Maybe Miss Vivee had said that the killer always came to the *funeral*. I shook off the thought, it was a distraction. I'm sure I had heard killers come back to the crime scene before, too.

Okay. *I'll just concentrate*, I thought. Quietly focus. See if I could identify the murderer.

I set my radar. *Beep, beep, beep* . . . I narrowed my eyes. "Beep, beep, beep." I scanned the perimeter and tried to peer deep into the mind of each spectator. Pick up any murderous thoughts . . . "Beep, beep, beep."

"Logan," Micah said my name jolting me from my concentrated efforts. He leaned over, a frown on his face. "What is wrong with you?"

"What?" I said and looked around, feeling a little embarrassed.

"You keep beeping," he said.

Chapter Seven

As usual, we didn't leave the crime scene until the body had been picked up, and as Miss Vivee put it, "carted away." We were in a southern town, I hadn't thought it stereotypical to note that most people had pick-up trucks, even if it wasn't their primary vehicle. I couldn't understand why the sheriff couldn't just pack the body up in any one of them. Miss Vivee had joked about it, but I wouldn't have minded if they used my jeep – let the backseats down and it could easily have accommodated the recently departed Kimmie Hunt. As long as someone detailed it afterward, it would have been fine with me.

But the coroner, after being fetched, returned and Kimmie had a proper, and official, transport to the morgue. Happily for me, there was no need to take her body up to Augusta, since (whew!) her death didn't appear to be out of the local Sheriff's jurisdiction. Bay was free from being a part of the investigation.

After putting Miss Vivee in the car, and getting her buckled in, Micah and my mother climbed in the back and we headed over to the Maypop. Finally. I couldn't wait to get a shower and something to eat.

"Oh what a beautiful house," my mother said as we drove up to the Maypop. "Kind of reminds me of my sister Claire's house. But much grander."

"Wait until you see inside, Mommy," I said.

"Yep. This is where your daughter sought refuge when she was running from the FBI," Miss Vivee said. "Ane we haven't been able to get her out of the house yet."

"And wait until you taste Renmar's cooking," I said ignoring Miss Vivee's comments. "She is the best around."

"Good," Micah said. "Because I'm starving. Where are all the McDonald's? I haven't seen one since we left the Airport."

"You'd have to leave Yasamee to find a fast food restaurant," I said.

"Well where'dya eat?" he asked.

"Here," I said turning the knob on the door to the bed and breakfast I called home. "We have a kitchen. Or at Jellybean's."

"Jellybean's?" he questioned. "Is that a candy store?"

"No," I said. "It's a diner."

As soon as I pushed the door open, Brie was standing there a smile so wide she was beaming, cradling something in her arms.

"Hi!" she said.

"Hello," my mother said, a look of curiosity on her face. "I'm Justin, Logan's mom."

"I know," Brie said excited. "I couldn't wait to meet you."

"Oh, Brie," Miss Vivee said. "What in the tarnation are you doing?"

"Momma," Miss Vivee's youngest child said, her eyes twinkling. "Do you know who this is?"

"Of course I do," she said. "Don't be ridiculous. This is Logan's mother."

Ever since I'd found out that Brie was dating Sheriff Lloyd Haynes, I had noticed how pretty she looked. Downplaying her fifty-something years, she no longer wore "grandmotherly" attire – thick soled shoes, crocheted sweaters, shift cotton dresses, her hair in a French roll – but had started putting on face powder to cover the sprinkle of freckles over her nose, her auburn frocks coiffed, and much more stylish clothes. But today, as she stood to meet my mother, she even looked radiant.

I couldn't understand what she could be so excited about.

"No," Brie said and bit her lip. "She's more than that." Then she stuck out a copy of my mother's book. "Can you sign this for me, please?"

It was the one she'd written about people coming from Mars.

I held my breath and looked over at my mother, then at my brother. I slid up next to him, thinking I might need him as a shield to my mother's ire. I wasn't sure how she would react, and I didn't know if she'd blame me for Brie knowing about the book. Maybe even thinking I gave it to her. It certainly wasn't a good subject to broach with my mother first thing.

"I'll be happy to," my mother said. Not even flinching.

I blew out my breath.

"Ma, this is Brie, Miss Vivee's daughter," I said. "And this is my brother, Micah."

"Nice to meet you, Brie," my mother said taking the book. Micah nodded. Brie just kept smiling and stuck out a pen.

"How about I do it over here?" My mother pointed to the registration counter that divided the foyer from the entrance and the rest of the house.

"Just write, 'To my cousin, Brie.'"

"Cousin?" my mother asked.

"Well, when Bay and Logan get married I'll be her aunt-in-law, and you and I'll be in-laws some kind of way, but I figured that be too much to write on here, don't you think?" My mother didn't say anything. "And down here *everybody* are cousins."

"'To my cousin, Brie' it is," my mother said, and scrawled it in the book.

"I thought I heard commotion out here," Renmar came around through the dining room. Following close behind was Hazel Cobb. "Well who do we have here?"

"Renmar Colquett, this is my mother, Justin, and my brother, Micah."

"Hi," my mother said.

"Mom, Renmar is Bay's mother. And this is Hazel Cobb, Bay's cousin on his father's side."

I thought it might be a little racist to point that out seeing Hazel was black, and it let people know that Renmar had married a black man. But that's how they always introduced Hazel, and no one seemed to mind. Plus, everyone could see that Bay was black and his mother wasn't.

"Nice to meet you," my mother said. "Nice to meet everyone."

"I'm a hugger," Hazel Cobb said and grabbed my mother, locking her in a tight squeeze.

"I was just fixing a little brunch for ya'll," Renmar said. "I hope ya'll are hungry."

"Yes ma'am," my rude brother, Micah said. He hadn't opened his mouth until that point. "I'm starving." He took in a whiff, and a smile spread across his face. "And it smells really good in here."

"You're always hungry," my mother said.

My brother was tall and skinny as a rail, even though he always had his nose in the refrigerator or his car in a drive-thru. He wore his hair cut low, and if he wasn't at work at the law firm my uncle owned, he was in a pair of jeans and a T-shirt. He probably had loads of money because he billed at $275 an hour for his sixty-hour week as an attorney and still lived with my parents, catching a ride to work with our uncle.

"Oh he's fine," Hazel Cobb said and waved her hand. "C'mere and give me a hug. Any family of Logan's is family to us, too."

"I can't take being in that big ole house anymore!" A very short, very loud woman came barreling through the door, tripping over her luggage as she pulled it behind her. Then she let out a wail that rivaled the doggie refrain I'd heard this morning. "Kimmie's dead!" she shrieked. "And it's all my fault!"

Chapter Eight

*Well that's a first,* I thought. *The murderer announcing it without anyone asking.*

Renmar rushed to her. "Frankie!" she said. "Are you okay?"

"No!" she cried out. "I'm not." She dabbed at her eyes, and sniffed. "Everything in that house reminds me of Kimmie and I just can't stay there any longer."

"Where's Nash?" Renmar asked.

"Down at the police station," she said. "He's camped out down there saying he's going to help the sheriff." She shook her head. "What does he think, this is the Old West? That they're just going to ride out at dawn and go and get their man?"

"Is it alright?" Brie asked.

"That man is healthy as a horse, strong as an ox, and frisky as a ferret. He'll be fine."

"It is his daughter," Renmar said, giving her a suspicious look.

Everyone stared at Frankie, and then Frankie let her eyes go to each one of ours before she let out another howl. "Kimmie!" she screamed and her knees buckled, I just knew she was going down.

Hazel Cobb grabbed her. "Frankie!" she said.

Renmar moved in and started fanning her with her hand. "Micah!" she directed. "Get a chair!" She pointed to the dining room.

"Oh my," my mother said and slid up next to me. "Who is that?" she whispered.

I hunched my shoulders. "I don't know."

Miss Vivee took my mother's hand and led her over to the beige tufted bench by the front door. It was me and Miss Vivee's usual hangout.

She sat, then pulled my mother down next to her. "That's Kimmie's mother," Miss Vivee said and leaned in closer. "Her *step*mother."

"Well why does she think she's responsible?" my mother asked. "Doesn't she know she was stung by a hornet?"

"She doesn't know much of anything," Miss Vivee said. "At least that's what she wants people to think."

"What makes you think that you're responsible for Kimmie, Frankie?" I heard Renmar ask after they'd gotten her stable. She had instructed Hazel Cobb to get a cold towel and Micah a glass of water out of the kitchen. She was standing next to Frankie's chair holding her hand.

"Because I shouldn't have let her go out running this morning. She likes to run around that square like it's a track." Frankie shook her head as if she didn't

4

understand the purpose of that. "She'd just gotten back into town, you know," she continued. "And had jet lag something fierce. She'd been on one of her trips. This time to China, and her last stop was India. She even had a small fever. No telling where she got that from. I made her put on that jogging suit," Frankie said all in one breath.

Micah had made it back with the water, spilling it as he came rushing back. Renmar held it while Frankie took time out from talking to take a sip. "I made her zip it up." Frankie swallowed the small amount of water with much to much effort, and continued talking. Looking at Renmar, tears spilling down her face, she said, "I just wanted her to keep warm."

"Well of course you did, Sweetie."

"She must have been sweating something awful," Miss Vivee whispered to me.

"Well, you can't hold yourself responsible because of that." Hazel Cobb said to Frankie as she returned with the cold compress. "She didn't die from being overheated."

"I should have been a better mother," Frankie said and hiccupped. "Insisted that she not go out."

"You couldn't have known," Renmar said holding the compress up to Frankie's head.

"You're probably right," Frankie said taking the rag from Renmar and dabbing her eyes with it. "But I just feel so awful."

"Well of course you do," Renmar said.

As she was recuperating, Miss Vivee gave us the lowdown on Frankie.

Her full name was Francesca Hunt, wife of Nash Hunt, who was Kimmie's father. She'd married Nash when Kimmie was eight. He'd bought Stallings Inn, a bed and breakfast a little larger than the Maypop, but not as old for the family to run. It was the only other place in Yasamee for travelers.

Miss Vivee said that everyone in town had gotten an earful from Frankie when she first arrived of how hard it was to be a stepmother and run a bed and breakfast in "little ole, not even on the map, Yasamee." But she said that Frankie soon mellowed out, and her complaints became few and far in-between. Still, sometimes at the beauty parlor, or in Hadley's drug store, Miss Vivee said, Frankie had been heard saying, "Even with the hard life," she'd been dealt, she was "an expert at putting on a brave face and carrying on. Thank God for Nash's money," she'd say, otherwise she told everyone she didn't know how she would've been able to "bear it."

I perused Frankie. That brave face, although now messy and tear stained, was made up in thick mascara, a touch of eye shadow and beet red lipstick. Just by looking at her, I could tell she was more sophisticated than most Yasamee-nites.

Frankie wore her nails long, and the same color as her lips. Her hair was a beautiful silver gray, and she wore it straight. Cut in angles around her jaw line,

5

1

parted on the side, her feathered bangs fell often into her face.

Then I looked at Miss Vivee and wondered how she'd know so much about Frankie when she had spent the twenty years prior to me coming inside the house.

*Miss Vivee probably just made that all up.*

I came back from my reverie just as Renmar took a step back from Frankie, shaking her head.

"Frankie," Renmar said. "I know you're in a tizzy right now, but the house is full because of the wedding and everything. I really don't have a room available for you to stay."

"Let your guests go over to Stallings Inn," Frankie said, her sobs growing stronger. "We'll take all your overflow."

"I really don't have *overflow*," Renmar said. "It's just we're all booked up."

"Well, unbook it!" Frankie squealed shaking her head like anyone would know that was the logical thing to do.

"If you're here," Renmar said, trying to be patient. "Who'll take care of the guests over there?"

"I don't know!" Her sobs reaching a crescendo. "All I know is that I can't."

"Frankie you have to be realistic," Renmar seem to plead with her.

"They can sleep there, at Stallings Inn, and come over here and eat," she said waving her hand in the air.

"Frankie -"

Frankie popped up from her seat. "They can stay at my inn for free," she said. She swiped the rag across her face, smearing all that was left of her make-up, and then blew her nose into the compress. Holding Renmar's hand open, palm up, with one of hers, she slammed the rag down into it. She hurled her purse down on the registration counter and started digging down in it.

"Here, take the keys," Frankie said and held them out to Renmar. And when Renmar didn't reach for them she flung them across the counter. "They can just let themselves in. I'll take the room off the kitchen." She gathered up her stuff. "You know, the old servant quarters. I know you still keep a bed back there." She sniffed, wiped her nose with her hand and picked up the handle or her roller luggage.

"I use that for storage." Renmar seemed flabbergasted and at a loss for words. "Really, Frankie," was all she could seem to say.

"However it looks is fine with me," Frankie said. "I don't care. Storage room or not."

"Renmar," Brie said. She'd been standing off in a corner and hadn't said a word the whole time. She did that sometimes, she could be totally uninvolved and uninterested even with the house falling down around her. "Just let her stay. She just lost her child."

Renmar looked at Frankie, over to us and back at Brie. She shook her head, closed her eyes, and let her

5

arms fall down. "Alright. She can stay." She looked at Frankie. "You can stay."

"Good," Frankie said. She took another sniff and tilted her head to the side, she suddenly seemed calm. "What is that heavenly smell?" she asked and headed off to the kitchen.

Chapter Nine

I always felt like I needed to best my mother. Once I had decided to become an archaeologist, she was the one to beat. Now it seemed as if I were competing against her sleuthing. I chuckled to myself.

*How in the world did she know that Kimmie Hunt was bitten by an Asian Hornet?*

There was so much still to learn from her. How could I think I could be better than her?

One thing my mother never did was jump to conclusion, and that's one trait I definitely could use.

After Francesca Hunt came over thinking that she'd killed Kimmie because she had made her put on that jogging suit, I started thinking. *Why in the world did I jump to the conclusion that Kimmie had been murdered?*

Kimmie had been stung by a hornet. An *Asian* hornet per my mother and Miss Vivee, and she'd just come from Asia. (Although I knew that didn't necessarily mean we didn't have the hornets here. We had *Brazil* nuts, and *French* fries.)

5

Sitting Indian style in the middle of my bed, after eating and taking a much needed shower, I decided I needed to learn more. I pulled out my laptop to Google the little bugger.

"Hey, what'chya doing?"

I looked up and saw my big brother standing in the doorway.

"Trying to figure out how Mommy knew what killed that girl."

"Your Miss Vivee knew too, aren't you curious how she figured it out?"

"No," I said. "She and Mac have a knack for that."

"Knack for what?" He plopped down on the bed. "They know about insect bites?"

"They know about everything when it comes to suspicious causes of death. At least with all the murders we've come across."

"And how many is that?" he asked.

"This makes number seven. But I was just thinking that maybe Kimmie Hunt wasn't killed"

"Seven?" He let out a whistle. "Girl, they don't keep that many bodies in a morgue at one time."

I laughed. "I believe it."

"So, what you find out?" he asked and pointed to my laptop.

"I was just getting started." I clicked on the one of the links and read out loud. "The hornet is attracted by human sweat," read the first line of the link I pulled up under my search of "death by hornet." "And disturbed by human activity (particularly running), the hornets vigorously defend their territory, chasing people up to 600 feet and stinging them multiple times with their very toxic venom." I looked at Micah. "That was from the story on how forty-two people in China had died from hornet stings."

"Wow," Micah said. "That's pretty scary. And pretty much what that lady said about what happened with that dead girl."

"Kimmie," I said. "Her name was Kimmie. And what lady?"

"Her mother, remember she said 'Kimmie' was out running, probably sweating up a storm."

"Oh yeah. I remember."

"No jogging for me while I'm here."

I laughed. "So, you scared another one might be out there with your name on it?"

"Maybe," he said. "I don't mind admitting when I'm afraid of something. Are those things all over Georgia?"

"I was just looking that up." I went back to reading the article I'd pulled up on my computer. "I don't think they are here," I said and pointed at my monitor. "This story just says hornet. I'm guessing since the people who wrote the article were in Asia, they wouldn't call it an *Asian* hornet."

"And you're guessing then that the hornets are only in Asia?"

"Yep. That's my first guess." I said and looked back down at the screen. I scrolled half the page. "Here it is," I said. "These giant hornets can be found

5

in the Primorsky Krai region of Russia, Korea, China, Taiwan, Indochina (region which consists of the countries Laos, Thailand, Cambodia, Myanmar and Vietnam), Nepal, India, and Sri Lanka. But it says that they are most common in rural areas of Japan." I lifted my head. "Doesn't say anything about Georgia. You feel safe now?"

"Funny."

I shut the top to my laptop. "Have you guys heard from Courtney?" I asked.

"Yeah. Right before we left," he said and smiled. "She called Mom and Dad to say she sends her love."

"She likes what she's doing, huh?"

Courtney was the oldest of us children. There were three years between her and Micah, only two between him and I. Following in the footsteps of one of my mother's brother and a sister, Courtney was a teacher, now living in Tanzania working with Teachers Without Borders.

"Yeah," he said and nodded. "But you know she would've come for your engagement and everything if she could have."

"I know," I said.

"I figured it's all good," he said. "You and Courtney leaving the nest, living somewhere else."

"Why?" I asked.

"Because, our parents are getting old now, and I'll be the one to take care of them. That means they'll leave me everything."

"Oh brother," I said. "Is that what you think about, Mommy and Daddy dying off?"

"And me getting all their stuff? Sometimes."

"I can't wait until Dad gets here so I can tell him what his son thinks of him."

He started laughing. "You better worry about what they think of you."

"What is that supposed to mean?" I asked. "Did they say something about me?" I would never want to disappoint my parents.

"No," he shook his head. "I haven't heard them say anything, yet."

"So what do *you* think about all of this?"

I didn't want him to think bad of my either.

"All of what?" he asked.

"My life here. The Maypop. Miss Vivee," I said.

"Your amateur sleuthing?" Micah asked.

"Yeah. All of it. What'ya think?"

"I think you're going a little stir crazy down here. Running around with old people chasing murderers. And beeping at crime scenes."

"That was the first time I ever did that," I said.

"What was that all about?"

"Nothing," I said. I'd rather not tell him if he was already thinking I was a bit looney. "Go ahead. Tell me what you think."

"I don't think that your parents are too happy about it."

"You just said that they hadn't said anything."

5

"They haven't. But they're probably thinking it. It's not what they planned for you, you know? It's not even what *you* planned for you."

"Yeah. I know all of that," I said and sighed. "And don't tell them all about my Sherlock Holmes antics, either, okay?"

"Whatever." He gave me a disapproving look. "How do you even make money?" he asked. "How do you live?"

"I was never going to make a lot of money in my chosen profession, anyway."

"That's true. Not by going on digs and stuff. But you could teach, or become the curator of a museum like Mom did."

"I don't want to do those things. I like excavating."

"Well, you're not even doing that," he said raising an eyebrow.

I let out a long sigh.

"And that Miss Vivee is something else," he said. "How old is she, anyway?"

"Who knows," I said and laughed. "Renmar told me it's impolite to ask a woman's age, and Miss Vivee swears she's over a hundred."

"Is she?"

"I don't know. I doubt it. I think she's in her nineties. Maybe *late* nineties, but not a hundred."

"She sure does get around well," Micah said. "Even for ninety-something. And she's 'spry' as Grammy would say."

"I know, right? And wait until you meet Mac. Except for his limp, he's just as 'young' as Miss Vivee."

"I hope I grow old that well," Micah said.

"Me too."

Micah sat quiet for a moment, as if he was contemplating something. "So. I know Dad's coming, and you are his 'little girl' and all, and he'll give you whatever you want, but I can help you if you need me to," he said.

"What are you talking about?"

"Like money. Do you need some money? I can lend you some."

"Lend me?" I said and laughed. "According to you, I don't have a boot to piss in or a window to throw it out of."

"What?" he laughed. "What does that mean?"

"No money. And no way to get any. So how you expect me to pay you back?"

"Ha. Ha," he chuckled. He sure was finding me funny. "Well, your, uhm, let's see . . . What do they call them down here? Your *beau*, soon to be *husband* has a little money, I'm figuring. You can get it from him to pay me back."

"I could get it from him in the first place. Or, like you said, from my 'Daddy' so I don't need you, or your money. And," I emphasized. "I don't need any money from anybody anyway. I have my own. I made money for my work on Stallings Island, and for finding that fish that was thought to be extinct. And I

6

1

earned a little for my time at Track Rock Gap. Plus I have my credit cards."

"Track Rock Gap? Isn't that the place you broke into?"

I rolled my eyes. "That has nothing to do with the money they paid me to excavate there."

"You have turned into an out-of-work archaeologist, turned criminal-slash-detective."

I wanted so bad to disagree with him. But it was the truth. That was my life.

*What in the world was I doing?*

I changed the subject. "You wanna ride into Augusta with me?" I rolled off the bed, straightened out my clothes, and went over to the mirror.

"We just came from Augusta. Plus, I have jet lag."

"Boy, you were on that plane for an hour, if that," I pushed up my hair, and twisted a couple of curls.

"One hour from Atlanta to here. Two hours from home to Atlanta and we had a layover. We were at the airport at four this morning."

"C'mon.' I turned to him. "I need to get a new phone."

"What happened to your phone?"

"Death by dog saliva."

"Gross."

"Right?" I said and laughed.

"Okay," he said. "I'll go. But I'm not going to be running up and down the road with you the whole time I'm here."

"This is just one time," I said and wrinkled my brow. "What are you talking about?"

"I know you. You probably have a ton of things still to get for the wedding," he said. "I'm not doing any shopping stuff."

I chuckled. "No one asked you to, and," I said, "I'm all ready for the wedding."

"Yeah, like I believe that." He shook his head. "And I know Ma will need something from the mall before it's all said and done. I should have ridden down here in the car with Dad."

"Oh my goodness," I said. "You're complaining about stuff that hasn't even happened yet. Calm down and enjoy being with your baby sister."

"Enjoy being with you?" He looked up at the ceiling. "Yeah. I can't ever remember a time when that happened," he said then looked at me and winked.

6

Chapter Ten

We left my mother with Miss Vivee. They were playing a game of putt-putt on the miniature golf course installed in the backyard of the Maypop. Then Miss Vivee explained, she planned on giving my mother a tour of her greenhouse and gardens.

I made Miss Vivee promise that she wouldn't tell my mother about me helping her solve the murders we'd been inundated with. Then I made her double promise she wouldn't mention anything about it being my destiny.

Miss Vivee made an "X" over her mouth then bounced the Scout's honor salute – right hand palm facing out, the thumb holding down the little finger – off the brow of her forehead.

I blew out a sigh of relief, and pulled Micah out the door.

We rode up to Augusta and chatted the entire time, mostly about his non-paying clients, who'd wake him up in the middle of the night with ideas about how to work their case. Not with any real legal remedies, he said, but from information they got off the Internet or on the TV. He said dealing with them had made him wish he'd become a ditch digger. He'd rather be stuck in a hole than deal with them.

Because of the age difference between my sister, Courtney and I, Micah had always been the one that was stuck taking care of me (although he did more irritating than nurturing). But that had made us close, and I knew him better than anyone. And one thing I knew for sure, Micah didn't have a lot of patience. He should have known that too. So why he'd chosen to go into a profession where he had to deal with people, who for the most part were going through rough times – needing an ear to listen, and a shoulder to lean on, was a mystery to me.

"There's a T-Mobile store in RadioShack," I said after arriving at the mall.

"How do you know?"

"I Googled it."

*Why would he think I'd drive all the way here and not know where I was going?*

This wasn't the first time I had to replace my phone since coming to Yasamee. The first time was when I had dropped it into a fruit cup Renmar had made. I had been startled by Bay, who at the time I only knew as the "FBI Guy." I thought he was on my trail for illegally trespassing on federal lands. I smiled at the memory.

"What are you grinning about," Micah asked, evidently noticing my unexplained smile.

"None of your business," I said. My lawyer brother, already making a comment about Track Rock Gap, didn't need to know I had any fond memories of my criminal activities.

"*Hmmp*," he grunted. "You're as crazy as your mother. Smiling about nothing."

"She's your mother, too," I said. I grabbed his arm and pulled him along as I walked. "I'm not sure where RadioShack is. I need to look at this store map." I had spotted the large display guide at the entrance to the mall, and luckily for us, I discovered I had parked at the entrance it was near. Okay," I said. "It's right over there." I pointed. "C'mon."

"How long are you going to be?" Micah asked following behind me reluctantly.

"I don't know," I said. "As long as it takes to get a phone."

"Okay, well, I'ma go find the food court."

"Why don't you just wait for me? I might want something from the food court."

"I don't want to stand around in RadioShack. It's takes a while to get a phone. I could be doing something else."

Men. They seem to hate any kind of shopping.

"Fine," I said. I knew "something else" only meant eating.

"Do you need me?" he asked.

"No." I shook my head. "I don't need you."

*He hadn't even bothered to ask if I wanted something.*

I shook my head. I couldn't figure out why I had asked him to come to the mall with me in the first place. I guess just the excitement of having my big brother with me in Georgia took over my good sense. He was a "brother" through and through. Whether he did it or purpose, or it just came naturally, he was always on the opposite side of what I thought, or what I wanted to do. All the time. How could I not remember that? I just always wanted to tell my parents on him. Tell them to make him stop like I used to do, but I was too old for that now, so most times I just punched him. That always blew off some of the frustration he caused me.

I knew that if I really needed something, he'd be right there. He would stay with me and endure whatever it was I wanted him to do. He had his own way of showing it, but I knew he loved me – a lot – and would go to the ends of the Earth to help or protect me. I also knew that it was because he loved me that he worried about me and wanted to make sure I did the right thing. To him it wasn't a good thing that I was almost thirty and wasn't working, didn't have my own place to live, and was running around with old people.

And I adored my big brother, and I wanted to make him proud of me.

*I have to do better,* I thought.

I watched Micah walk aimlessly down the mall and head in the opposite direction of the Food Court clearly marked by huge signs.

*Wonder how long he'll be lost.* I looked at the T-Mobile stand right inside the door of RadioShack. No other customers were there. I knew it wouldn't take me long.

*I'll probably have to go and find him,* I thought as I saw him disappear around a corner.

*Geesh.*

I gave the RadioShack clerk my phone number, driver's license, and picked out a phone. I drummed my fingers on the counter as he called in my information and downloaded the data from my old phone to the new one. I looked out toward the mall and back at the clerk taking his time getting my new phone operable. My stomach started rumbling.

*I wish I had told Micah to bring me something back.*

Finally, the clerk handed me my phone, my ID, and a small shopping bag with the phone's accessories in it.

"Thank you," I said as he left to take care of another customer. I laid my wallet on the counter, opened it and started to put my driver's license away when I heard a low voice, close to my ear, its tone acerbic saying something to me.

"You have something that belongs to us," he said.

"What?" I said and spun around. A man, dressed in dark blue skinny jeans, and a black button-down shirt stood next to me. He swung his head, throwing his shiny black hair from his eyes and stared at me.

I turned around to see if perhaps he was talking to someone behind me, then back to him. "You talking to me?" He tilted his head. I thought I saw a faint smile come on his face. "I don't know what you're talking about," I said and shook my head. I looked around again to see who the "we" included. "I don't have anything of yours. Or of anyone else's."

"I saw you pick it up. Right next to that girl. You know, that *dead* girl." He gave a nod, and slowly walked past me. Deliberate like. Never taking his thin, hooded eyes off me. But, once he got on my other side, he looked past me and his taunting gaze disappeared. I turned to see what it was he'd seen. It was Micah coming back from the food court. When I turned back, he was gone. Micah may have been skinny, but he was muscular, and with his height he could appear menacing.

"Did you see that guy?" I asked Micah when he walked up.

"What guy?" he said and took a bite of his soft pretzel.

"That guy who was standing here next to me."

"No," he said, his mouth full. "I didn't see nobody." He raised an eyebrow. "You still trying to talk to guys? I thought you were getting married?"

I rolled my eyes. "Never mind," I said shaking it off.

*That guy must be crazy*, I thought.

Micah took a sip of his giant-sized lemonade and then another chunk of the pretzel, gobbling down half of it in the one bite.

"Did you get me anything?" I asked.

"No." He frowned. "You could buy your own if you had a job."

"I do have a job."

"What job?"

*Okay, so I didn't have a job.*

"I can afford to buy myself a pretzel," I changed my retort.

"Only if you can pay for it with a credit card," he said.

"I'm going to get a job," I said. "And I'll buy my own pretzel and pay for it however I choose."

"Good. Get a job." He smirked. "Then you can buy me a pretzel, too," he said and stuffed the last of it in his mouth. "'Cause I could really eat another one. I'm starving."

*I hope he chokes on that pretzel,* I thought eyeing him chomping down on his mouthful.

"Well. What are we waiting on?" he asked still chewing. "Did you get your phone?"

"Yes. I got it." I grabbed my bag off the counter and held it up so he could see.

"So, let's go," he said. "You don't need anything else, do you?"

"No. We can go," I said. I stuck my wallet in my pocket and took one last look around for Crazy Guy.

Chapter Eleven

Frankie had taken over Renmar's kitchen, and she had only been there half a day. She was baking, taking special orders from customers, and even had a petition going around to add lunch and dinner service to the menu. Everyone knew that the Maypop only served breakfast and dessert, unless it was Friday, then their patrons got lunch.

And much to Renmar's chagrin, she was schmoozing with the guests, buzzing around from table to table.

Micah and I got back from the mall and found my mother and Miss Vivee seated in the dining room.

"Did you get your phone?" my mother asked.

"Yep." I held up my shopping bag.

"Good thing you had insurance," she said. "Did you have fun, Micah?"

"At the mall?" he asked as if she couldn't have thought that.

"With your sister," she said.

He shook his head again as if he couldn't believe she could think that. I punched him and he chuckled.

7

1

"Okay, I'm going to find something to eat. Is it okay if I go back to the kitchen?" He pointed toward the back of the house and looked at Miss Vivee. She nodded.

I slid into the seat opposite my mother. "What you guys been up to?" I asked.

"Watching her," my mother said quietly and pointed with her head toward Frankie. "She hasn't sat still all morning."

"She was gallivanting all over the globe," Frankie was waving her hands around speaking to a table full of guests. "Like those Harlem Globetrotters. Only she wasn't from Harlem." Frankie tilted her head and blinked her eyes. "And she didn't play basketball." She slung her hands on her hips. "And she wasn't black." Frankie waved her hands as if it didn't matter that her analogy wasn't any good. "But isn't it nice that she can – could – enjoy her young life like that?" Everyone at the table nodded. "Which is good, 'cause as ya'll know she got started off like a herd of turtles." They all laughed, apparently understanding what she meant.

"Poor little Kimberly," Miss Vivee leaned in and whispered. "Stuck with a crazy stepmother."

My mother laughed. "A love hate relationship," she said. "Just like Logan and I have."

"Ma," I said. Didn't want her airing our dirty laundry, Miss Vivee didn't need any more ammunition to use against me, she gave me enough grief already.

"Same with the two of us," Miss Vivee said nodding her head. "I think she's just hard to get along with."

*Now they're just ganging up on me.*

"Yeah, but at least she isn't keeping secrets from you," my mother said.

"Secrets?" I said. "What are you talking about?"

"Miss Vivee told me how you've been down here solving murders. That's why you haven't been out on any digs."

"I have not," I said.

I didn't know why I lied like that.

"So are you saying that Miss Vivee isn't telling the truth?" My mother lifted an eyebrow.

I wanted to say so badly that it wouldn't be the first time Miss Vivee lied. In fact, for Miss Vivee it was a full-time pastime. I took in a breath, and instead said, "I was going to tell you about it. But there have just been so many things going on."

My mother gave me a look that told me we'd talk about it later.

I don't know why that made me nervous. I was nearly thirty. But our parents had been so good to the three of us, putting us all through college and then grad school for me, law school for Micah. No matter how old a child gets, I guess, they don't want to disappoint their parents.

"Your mother has agreed to help us solve Kimmie's murder," Miss Vivee said.

7

I gave Miss Vivee that same I'll-talk-to-you-later look I had gotten from my mother.

I looked over at Frankie flitting from table to table and remembered what she'd said. "We don't know that it was *murder*, Miss Vivee."

"You know it is." Miss Vivee narrowed her eyes at me. "Don't act like that because your mother's here."

"Act like what?" I asked.

"Persnickety."

Mouth dropped open, I started to say something. Instead, I shut it and clicked my teeth together. I took in a calming breath as to not sound "persnickety," whatever that meant.

"I don't even know what that word means," I finally said.

"Look it up in your Funky Wagnall's," she said.

My mother started laughing. "That's funny, Logan," she said and nudged me. "You get it? It's really Funk *and* Wagnall's."

*How am I going to deal with the both of them at the same time . . .*

"I don't know what that is either," I said.

"All she knows is Google, Miss Vivee," my mother said and reached over and patted my hand.

"Like I said, it might not be murder," I wanted to get the conversation back on track and away from me.

"Oh, we didn't tell you," Miss Vivee said. "While you were at the mall, the Sheriff came by. He was looking for Bay."

I held my breath. I wasn't sure I wanted to hear what was coming next.

"He said that Kimmie was murdered."

"He said," my mother said respectively over talking Miss Vivee, "that he couldn't say it wasn't murder. At least not right now. He was concerned that if Kimmie did die from being stung by an Asian Hornet, he didn't want to rule homicide out until he could find how the insect got in Yasamee."

"Right," Miss Vivee said nodding her head in agreement. "She was murdered."

My mother closed her eyes and chuckled. I chuckled too, but what I found humorous was knowing my mother would soon learn all about Miss Vivee and what a handful she really was.

"So, if I am going to help you solve Kimmie's murder like you've asked," my mother said. "I'll need to know something about her."

"See," I said. "That's exactly how I got roped into this stuff." I looked at Miss Vivee. "Her innocent charm."

"I think it'll be fun. Doing a little sleuthing. And Miss Vivee explained that the Sheriff actually asks for her help, and that we'd be able to get it all done before the wedding."

"You said that before, Miss Vivee," I said. "You couldn't think that you can solve this is three days?"

"Love will conquer all," she said with a nod. "Come Hell or high water we're having a wedding on Sunday."

7

5

I shook my head and looked at my mother. "The Sheriff only asked for Miss Vivee's help once," I said. "When they had a note with flowers on it and needed her to see if any of those flowers could have killed the victim. Other times she just stuck her nose in and dragged me and Mac along."

"However it happened," Miss Vivee said. "My input has been invaluable."

*I couldn't argue with that.*

"So you don't think it'll be okay?" my mother said and looked at me. "I wouldn't want to come down here and cause any trouble."

I looked at Miss Vivee who looked at me. I shook my head. "You can't mess with destiny, I guess. And this is what this seems to be turning out to be. It'll be fine, Mom," I said and threw up my hands. "So," I said to Miss Vivee, "what do you want to do first?"

"Now you're talking," Miss Vivee said.

## Chapter Twelve

Before she could sit through what she thought would be Miss Vivee's plan of action, my mother excused herself to go to the bathroom.

"Why did you tell my mother about that destiny stuff?" I said once my mother got out of earshot. "Me and you solving murders."

"She asked me," Miss Vivee said.

That answer was almost laughable. I wanted to be mad, but she acted so innocent and her face looked remorseful. Plus, I could see it was going to be hard to get a straight answer from her.

"She did not ask you, Miss Vivee," I said. "Why would she have asked you something like that? She didn't know anything about it. And you swore that you wouldn't tell her."

"I did no such thing," Miss Vivee said. "I'd never swear to anything and then go back on my word. It's nothing a lady would ever do."

"You did swear," I said. "Scout's honor? Three fingers and a salute?" I mimicked what she had did early.

"Is that what that means?" she asked, face frowned up.

"What did you think it meant?"

"I didn't know. It just seemed the right thing to do with you acting nervous and all. But, whew!" She swiped her hand across her forehead. "At least I didn't break a promise. I would have felt so bad."

"You did, Miss Vivee. You did break your promise."

"No," she said, extra crinkles lining her forehead. "I was never a Scout so that little ditty thing with my hand," she repeated the motion. "Didn't mean anything to me."

I rolled my eyes.

"What did I miss," my mother said as she sat back at the table. "You guys didn't start strategizing without me, did you?"

"Don't worry, Mommy. You didn't miss anything. Miss Vivee never has a plan."

"I do too," she said. "It's just that it kind of falls into place as we go along. You know. Gathering clues."

"Gathering clues?" my mother smiled. "Now that sounds like fun." She winked at me.

*Maybe she won't fuss at me too much about abandoning my career as an archaeologist because she seems to really be enjoying this.*

"So tell me about our victim, Kimmie," she said.

"'Kimmie?'" Miss Vivee said with a "*hmpf.*" "Her name was Kimberly." Miss Vivee scrunched her nose.

"Kimberly Hunt. Perfectly good name, why shorten it?"

*Didn't everyone call her Vivee? Short for Vivienne?*

Miss Vivee's set of standards were vast and ever evolving, and they never applied to herself. Only to others.

"I don't know much about her," Miss Vivee said finally answering my mother's question. "But we'll find out about her as we investigate." She nodded her head. "The first thing we do is talk to the people that might have means, motive and opportunity."

"Means, motive, opportunity," my mother repeated her words. "I've heard that on television before."

"See," Miss Vivee said. "That just goes to show solving murders isn't complicated. It's universally understood. Stick with me," she jabbed my mother in her arm, "and you'll learn quickly that there's nothing new under the sun, only the way you apply that knowledge." Miss Vivee looked at me. "So. Now. What about September Love?"

"Seppie?" I asked. "What about her?"

"She had opportunity," Miss Vivee said.

"She was hysterical," I said. "She wasn't even sure that Kimmie was dead."

"Doesn't mean she didn't do it," Miss Vivee said. "All that hysteria could have been a distraction to get you off her trail, in which case it worked. Or, it could have been that she instantly regretted doing it."

7

"She did have dogs that were quite agitated," my mother said. "They may have seen something that upset them."

"Like a murder," Miss Vivee said.

"Like a murder," my mother agreed.

"She was a bad dog walker," I said. "That's all there was to it. She didn't have any control over them. It was not because they witnessed her taking a hornet and sticking it to Kimmie Hunt."

"And she was out early," Miss Vivee said not paying any attention to how illogical that sounded.

"That's opportunity," my mother concluded seemingly following Miss Vivee's reasoning.

"She is definitely a suspect," Miss Vivee said.

"Definitely," my mother echoed.

I flapped my arms. Why do I even try to reason with Miss Vivee, and now my mother, too?

"So what does that mean?" I asked Miss Vivee as if I didn't already know.

"I think it's time to go and visit our first suspect."

"Our only suspect," I mumbled.

"She's not our only suspect," Miss Vivee said.

"Who else is a suspect?"

"Who else was out there," she said.

"Not me," I said shaking my head. "I know you are not talking about me."

"You were out there, but I don't think you'd kill Kimberly Hunt and then go and tell on yourself," Miss Vivee said. "Even if you are a bit slow at times."

"Then who?" I asked, ignoring her comment about my intelligence or lack thereof.

"Mac."

"Mac?" my mother and I said it together.

'Why you two seem so surprised?" Miss Vivee said. "He's under a lot of stress, and he could have just snapped." She mimicked breaking a stick in half.

"Oh brother," I said and rolled my eyes.

"Well, you're the one who said it, Missy."

"Said what?"

"You're the one who told me he was out early, very early I might add. *Supposedly* waiting for the florist shop to open so he could buy a boutonnière when all the time he knew I already had one for him. Who sits on a bench for two hours? And you said he was acting melancholy."

"I never used that word," I said.

"It's what you meant," Miss Vivee said. "You said he hadn't seemed too surprised to hear Kimberly Hunt was dead, and he hasn't been around since it happened."

"It just happened this morning," I said. "And he came to get you."

"He thought with me on the trail, once I found out he was the murderer, I'd help him get away with it."

My mother chuckled. I just shook my head. Miss Vivee could spin gold out of straw.

"Why would he kill Kimmie Hunt," I asked.

8

1

"I don't know," Miss Vivee said. "We'll have to find out. But first stop is Seppie Love's house." She looked at my mother. "You in?"

"I'm in," she said.

"I stood up. "I'll get the car. And just so you know . . . So *both* of you know, I whole-heartedly disagree with Seppie Love or Mac being a suspect."

"That's the reason I run this show," Miss Vivee said. "I'm the only one with any far-sightedness."

*No,* I thought, *it's because you're the only one that can come up with any far-fetched-ness ideas.*

## Chapter Thirteen

I didn't know if that radar power I'd thought I might be developing was a true thing or not – beeping aside – but I definitely didn't get any kind of "vibe" from September Love.

And I didn't need any kind of power to know that Mac hadn't had anything to do with it.

Seppie had been gone by the time Miss Vivee got there, I was sure of that. She hadn't wanted to stay when Mac and I left her. So there wasn't anything Seppie could have done to make Miss Vivee see her as a suspect. But I also knew that following Miss Vivee's machinations always led to the killer. So, I got everyone into my jeep – Miss Vivee in front, my mother in the back –and pulled out of the driveway ready to follow Miss Vivee's crooked road of inquiry.

"Where to, Miss Vivee?" I was sure she knew where September Love lived. She knew where everyone lived.

"Don't you just hate this truck?" Miss Vivee said to my mother instead of answering my question. "I have to climb into it like I'm going up the side of a mountain, and then it sits up so high." She wiggled around in her seat.

"Yes," my mother said. "My husband has an SUV and I refuse to ride in it. I have a sedan."

"Me too!" Miss Vivee said and tried to turn around in her seat to look back at my mother. Her five-foot nothing frame too old to maneuver around. "But Logan refuses to drive it."

"She has a boat, Ma," I said. "It just so happens to have four wheels."

"They don't make cars like mine anymore," Miss Vivee said, giving a firm nod.

"For good reason," I said. "Now you wanna tell me which way to go to get to your suspect's house?"

"Go that way," Miss Vivee pointed and I took off. All set to find Kimmie's killer.

No more than ten minutes later, we pulled up in front of a beige house with green shutters. The windows were opened wide, and I could see the sheer curtains floating in the breeze. The front door stood ajar and the only thing protecting it from people wandering right in was a screen door. On the small porch a wind chime that read "Welcome" clinked in the calm wind.

"So what's the plan?" my mother asked.

"I usually do all the talking," Miss Vivee said. "But if you feel the need, just jump right in."

*Oh goodness,* I thought. *She's gonna let my mother talk? She never lets me say anything.*

"Miss Vivee?" September said pushing the screen door open after we knocked. She had two cats at her feet, one Calico, the other a white Persian. "Oh my goodness, it is you. I thought by now you'd be-"

"Dead?" Miss Vivee said.

"I didn't mean-"

"Well I will probably die if I have to stand at this door much longer. Where are your manners?"

"Oh I'm sorry," she said. "Ya'll come on in." We went through the door single file and when I walked past Seppie she said my name.

"Logan. What are you doing here?" She seemed as if it were a pleasant surprise.

"That's my granddaughter," Miss Vivee said.

"Granddaughter?" Then recognition lit up her eyes. "You're married to Bay?"

"Not yet. So don't get any ideas," Miss Vivee said. "It's practically a done deal. Show her the ring."

I held up my hand.

"I never had any-" September started.

"Designs on my grandson?" Miss Vivee asked.

*Is Miss Vivee going to let her finish a sentence?*

September started to say something, but I knew how defensive and protective Miss Vivee was about Bay, so I interrupted. No need getting our "suspect" more upset than she was.

"This is my mother, Justin," I said and pointed.

8

5

"What's going on?" a man's voice came from behind us. I turned around to see a young guy, dressed in jeans, barefoot and pulling an olive green T-shirt over his head and down around his six-pack stomach.

"This is Keith Collier," September said and gestured toward the guy. "A friend of ours."

"Ours?" Miss Vivee asked.

"Me and . . . Uhm . . . Me and Kimmie's." She lowered her head and bit her bottom lip that I noticed was trembling.

I felt bad for Seppie. I knew how upset she'd been about Kimmie's death, and now to be interrogated by the likes of us. I watched her as she stood fiddling with the bottom of her shirt, tears rolling down her face.

She was a pretty girl. Big baby doll eyes, full lips, and smooth skin gave her the look of a model. She wore her hair short, with bouncy ringlets. She had long, skinny legs that had been hidden under the jeans she had on when I'd seen her earlier. Now she had on shorts, and it was obvious she was nervous – pulling on her Daisy Duke's and crossing and uncrossing her legs. She looked like a flamingo.

I looked down at her feet and thought she must have passed those feelings of tension on to her cats because they were making figure eights around her legs and purring.

"Are you okay, Seppie?" Keith Collier asked. He stood in the archway that separated the hallway and the room we were in. Seppie nodded, but didn't say anything. Then she looked back over at us standing around.

"Oh. Please, have a seat," she said. "I don't know what I'm thinking." She pushed some clothes off the couch and spread her arm out gesturing us to sit. The three of us sat on it, with me in the middle.

As soon as we sat both cats went straight to Miss Vivee.

"What's your cats' names?" Miss Vivee asked.

I knew she was being nice now only to soften the blow, because I had a feeling she wasn't going to show Seppie any mercy when she started her questions.

"The white one is Whiskers, and the Calico is Paws."

"Not very original, huh?" Miss Vivee said. Seppie hunched her shoulders. "I have a dog," Miss Vivee continued. "She's a wheaten Scottish terrier."

"What's her name?" Seppie asked, her face brightening.

"Cat," Miss Vivee said.

Seppie laughed and looked at me. "Really?" she said.

"Really," I said.

"How cute," she said.

"Seppie," I said. I figured I'd maybe ask the questions. I knew I wouldn't be as harsh. "I was wondering. Did you see a black car this morning?"

"You mean the one that the dogs almost ran into?"

That was a good way to put it, I thought, because that car had been moving so slowly that it wouldn't have hit them.

"Yeah, I saw it," she said. "Why? Because what about it?"

"I don't know," I shrugged. "Seeing you again just made me think of it. And it seemed strange. I've never seen it before. And it seemed to just be hanging around, you know? Like it was up to something."

"I haven't ever seen it either," she said. "Is that who you think killed Kimmie?"

"How do you know she was killed?" Miss Vivee asked.

"Because . . ." Seppie looked at me, then back at Miss Vivee. "I saw her . . . I mean the way she was just lying there. You know." She swiped a tear from her eye. "Her face . . . Her face didn't look like she had had a heart attack or anything."

"Were you and her still close?" Miss Vivee asked.

Seppie looked at Keith Collier who was still standing in the doorway to the living room. He hadn't said a word, but when her eyes met his, he looked away, then turned around and went back wherever it was he had hailed.

"Yes," she said turning back to face us. "We were still friends," she said and plopped down in a chair across from us. She looked at Miss Vivee. "So then, if she wasn't killed, do they know how she died?"

"No," Miss Vivee said. My mother looked at me out of the corner of her eye. "You know it takes a long time for them to do an autopsy," Miss Vivee continued with the deception. "Don't you watch television?"

"I . . . I hadn't . . . I didn't know," she stumbled over her words. "Everything you see on television isn't real anyway."

"Yes, I guess you're right," Miss Vivee said. "But they'll find out soon enough. Bay's on the case. And it won't be long after, if they determine there was foul play, that they'll catch whoever did it."

"I heard Bay was with the FBI," she said a lopsided grin crawling up her face, evidently Miss Vivee's accusation going right over her head. Then she caught herself and looked at me. "That's just what I heard."

"So what do you know about it?" Miss Vivee asked.

"Me?" Seppie's eyes got even bigger than they were naturally.

"Yes you," Miss Vivee said. "You were at the town square this morning."

"I was walking dogs."

"So you say," Miss Vivee said, a smirk on her face.

"I was," Seppie said sitting up straight. "She saw me." She pointed to me. "Logan saw me."

"No need having a hissy," Miss Vivee said. "We're just trying to help ole' Nash Hunt. You know he's taking all this real hard."

"Oh," Seppie said as if she'd just realized that Kimmie's death had affected others. "He was already sick, I know this'll just kill him." Then she grabbed her mouth like she had said something she wasn't supposed to say.

"He was sick?" Miss Vivee asked catching Seppie's reaction.

"I really shouldn't say anything." Miss Vivee eyed September, giving her a You'd-Better-Tell-What-You-Know-Or-Else look. Seppie cleared her throat and complied. "That's what Kimmie had told me. That he wasn't feeling well. But, I don't know that for sure."

"Well it's what he has told me, too."

*There she goes with her lies.* Miss Vivee, I knew, hadn't spoken with Nash Hunt.

"I just wasn't sure if you knew about it or not," she continued

"He did?" Seppie tilted her head surprised Miss Vivee knew and seemingly relieved she hadn't been the one to spill the beans. "I didn't know he spoke about it. Kimmie had told me not to tell anyone."

"Well you didn't do a good job of that," Miss Vivee said raising her eyebrows. "What if we hadn't already known?"

*Which we didn't.*

"But Nash told me," Miss Vivee said, "because he wanted me to help find out what happened to Kimmie. You know I'm the one who figured out who killed Gemma Burke."

"That was you?" Seppie asked her and smiled. "I just figured Sheriff-"

"Well of course it was his case," Miss Vivee said. "But he counts on me to help." Now she was starting with her tall tales. "And I'm trying to help now."

"When did Kimmie get back?" my mother asked.

*Good. Finally questions that could help find out what happened.*

"Back?"

"Yes. Hadn't she taken a trip?"

"Oh yeah," she said and laughed. "She was always going somewhere. She had just gotten back a couple of days ago. Wait. Yesterday." She nodded. "Yeah, it was just yesterday. She came, you know, to see about her father. She said she would've stayed longer but . . ." September seemed to have remembered something. She fixed her eyes on the floor and let her words drift.

"I've promised Nash I'd help the Sheriff," Miss Vivee said. She must've noticed that Seppie's thoughts had wafted. "You want to help, too, don't you?" she asked. "Seems like you keep trying to keep secrets. That won't help you know."

Seppie took in a deep breath. "I got this postcard from her." Seppie lifted her eyes from the floor and looked at Miss Vivee. "From Kimmie. I didn't know if she was telling me the truth or not. She liked to play practical jokes." She shook her head. "She learned it from Mrs. Hunt, you know?"

"Frankie?" Miss Vivee said.

"Oh. Yeah. Frankie. Well I call her Mrs. Hunt. Anyway when we were young, Kimmie and I, Mrs. Hunt used to always play practical jokes on us. It was really kind of annoying." Seppie doe-like eyes looking past us, as if remembering. "Then when we got older, Kimmie started to do them too. You know, pull pranks. Even though she never liked it."

"A postcard?" I said. That seemed anachronistic to me. Kimmie was young, surrounded by technology. I just didn't see someone in our generation using snail mail. Why wouldn't she just send her an email?

September must have read my thoughts. "Kimmie said she thought someone might hack her computer," she said and chuckled. "And, that might have been part of her prank. I don't know. You know, to make it seem more ominous. More like a mystery."

"What was the prank?" I asked.

"That she'd found something. Something valuable. In India," she said looking at me.

"What did she find?" Miss Vivee asked.

September hunched her shoulders. "Some guy thousands of years ago wrote about some Christian relics he'd found in India. It's in the bible." She looked up at us. "Or at least that's what Kimmie wrote in her postcard."

"And she has it?" I asked.

"I don't know." September closed her eyes and sighed. "I don't know." She opened her eyes back up and looked at me. "That's what I thought, once I read it. That she had it. But that would be something really important, right? How would *she* have it?"

"Bar-Daisan," my mother said.

"What is that, Mommy?"

"It's a who. A man. Lived around 154-223 BC. He wrote that Christian tribes had been found in North India supposedly converted by Thomas." My mother shook her head like it was unbelievable. "Well that's the short version of it. I dug there once. Well. I helped a colleague. It was so hot." She seemed to now be talking more to herself than to us. Thinking through what she knew. "There are believed to be books and relics to prove the existence of Christians in India. If that is what she has that would be an important find."

"How do you know that's what Kimmie meant, Ma?" I said. The archaeologist in me not wanting to jump to any conclusions. "That's not a lot of information to go on to make such a conclusion."

"It's not a lot of Christians in India, especially thousands of years ago," she said speaking from her years working as a Biblical archaeologist. "And there are no – zero – Indians in the Bible. She would have had to have been talking about the Acts of Thomas, a non-canonized book. Bardaisan is believed to have written one hundred-fifty psalms, imitating David's, that are in Thomas' epistle. And he supposedly wrote about Christians in India as well, but all that work is lost. There might be proof of it somewhere, but nothing has ever been found. Unless," she looked at me, "Kimmie found it."

3

"Do you believe there were really a tribe of Christians in India?" Miss Vivee asked.

"Never found anything to prove it true. Never found anything to prove it not true. On that dig anyway," my mother said. "But. Yes. I've read parts of Thomas attributed to Bardaisan. Beautiful lyrics. So he existed. He wrote about Christianity. He went to India." My mother hunched her shoulders. "So him knowing something about Christians in India is not a far-fetched notion."

"But Kimberly Hunt having such a relic is far-fetched," Miss Vivee said.

"I guess," my mother didn't want to close the possibility by agreeing with that. Knowing her she'd need more facts before forming any type of conclusion.

"Well, if she did have it," Miss Vivee said. "Or something she claimed to be it, she would've gotten it illegally and that would have potentially been a dangerous thing for her."

"A very dangerous thing," my mother said knowingly. She'd been in enough hot water for having ancient relics that other people wanted.

"Well isn't that September Love a little hot momma," Miss Vivee said when we all got into the car after our visit with Seppie.

*Hot momma?* I saw my mother in the rearview mirror mouth the words.

"What does that mean, Miss Vivee?" I asked reaching over and buckling her seat belt.

"That was Kimmie Hunt's boyfriend standing in that doorway half naked."

"He wasn't half naked," I said. "And how do you know? You spent the last twenty years inside your house, I'm sure you've never seen him."

"If you didn't notice how much that Francesca Hunt talks, you'll never make a good detective," Miss Vivee said.

My eyes shot to the mirror to see what my mother's reaction to those words were. *Detective.* I was sure she wouldn't be okay with me being called that.

"So is that how you knew about Keith, Miss Vivee?" my mother asked not reacting to her comment. "Mrs. Hunt told you?"

"She told everybody," Miss Vivee said and waved her hand. "The woman can't keep her mouth shut. So now what is he doing there with September Love?"

I turned and looked at my mother and then at Miss Vivee and shrugged. "I don't know," I said. And it seemed my mother didn't have an answer either.

"Well, I know what he's doing," Miss Vivee said. "It's called *collusion.*" She gave a resolved nod of her head. "I'd say that this turn of events is worthy of telling the Sheriff. And Bay."

*Oh no. Not Bay,* I thought.

"I'm sure the Sheriff has questioned her, Miss Vivee," my mother said. She hadn't gotten to know Miss Vivee too well. Yet.

"Miss Vivee thinks that she is the one who is supposed to tell the Sheriff, *and* Bay, what to look for, and what to do."

"I'm sure that's not what she thinks," my mother said.

"Ask her," I said.

"Do you?" my mother asked.

"Do I what?" Miss Vivee said coyly.

My mother chuckled.

Miss Vivee looked at me. "You call them."

"And tell them what?" I said looking at my mother in the mirror.

"That he needs to check out those two." She jerked her thumb back toward the house we were still sitting in front of.

"See, Ma," I said. "I told you."

"Well what are you waiting on?" Miss Vivee said.

"Okay. I'm calling," I said with a grin, and pulled out my phone.

"And tell them *everything* that Seppie told us."

"Okay."

"Call the Sheriff first," Miss Vivee directed.

"Okay," I said.

"And stop saying 'okay.'"

I looked at her and smiled.

I called the Sheriff and relayed our conversation with Seppie, including, after Miss Vivee practically poked a hole in my side with her finger, Keith Collier being there and all about the postcard. After I finished, he had me put the phone on speaker so Miss Vivee could hear.

"Miss Vivee, you're not trying to solve my case, are you?"

"Yes I am," she said.

"Well don't. It's my job. I can do it without your help."

"I'm only doing it because Mac is a suspect."

"Mac Whitson?"

"Do you know any other Mac?" Miss Vivee asked.

"Mac is not on my suspect list, Miss Vivee," the Sheriff said.

"Well, he's on mine," Miss Vivee said.

"Put Logan back on the phone," he said. "And take me off of speaker."

I gave my mother a look through the rearview mirror that said, "I told you so."

When I got off the phone, after listening to the Sheriff telling me repeatedly not to let Miss Vivee get involved, and how he was going to have a talk with Bay, I turned to Miss Vivee and opened my mouth to relay the conversation to her.

"I don't care what he says," Miss Vivee said, holding up her hand. "He can't tell me what to do."

And how well did I know that!

It was impossible to get Miss Vivee to conform to any directive she was given. She did just what she

9

wanted to do. And for some reason, even after knowing all of that, I still seemed to just follow blindly behind her.

"So where to now, Miss Vivee?" my mother asked.

*And now, it seems, so does my mother.*

I think we need to go to Jellybean's," Miss Vivee said. "But first I want you to stop at Hadley's," she looked at me, "and get me a notebook and-"

"Two No. 2 pencils." I finished her sentence. "I already know."

Chapter Fourteen

"Oh what a delightful little place," my mother said. Smiling she looked at Miss Vivee. "Do you two come here often?"

"Only when there's a crime to be solved," Miss Vivee said. "It's usually the three of us – me, Mac, and Logan."

The diner really was where we came to discuss the murder of the day, even the owner, Viola Rose had caught on to that. Only this time it was me, my mom, Micah and Miss Vivee.

Micah wasn't really included in our little gumshoe operation we'd formed, but when Miss Vivee suggested we go to the Café, I knew I couldn't go to a place that served food and not pick up my brother. Because I figured, as he always said, he was "starving."

We had walked into Munchkinland, otherwise known as Jellybean's Café, and waited to be seated. It was a bright and colorful place – white floors, walls, and table tops, with a punch of color – orange, purple, yellow and red cushions – for the stools and benches.

9

Dazzling neon signs in all the windows, an aroma of good food that brought patrons in by the droves. I'd stopped at Hadley's as instructed, and Miss Vivee was holding onto her plastic bag filled with her sleuthing paraphernalia. I knew she couldn't wait to get started.

"And where is this mystery man of yours, Miss Vivee?" my mother said as we waited to be seated. "I'd have thought I would have met him by now. Logan has told me so much about him."

"I don't know," Miss Vivee said. "He's done gone and disappeared on me. A tendency murder suspects have."

"Miss Vivee," I said.

"But don't worry, he'll be at the wedding, even if he's in handcuffs. You can bank on that."

"Well, I hope so," my mother said and chuckled. "Wouldn't be a celebration without him."

I was worried about Mac. Miss Vivee didn't seem to be, though. She even had him as a suspect. Mac had been absent, and unlike Miss Vivee, I was concerned that maybe he wouldn't show up for the ceremony. I remembered he told me when I found him at the florist shop that he hadn't wanted to see Miss Vivee. I'd never known him to say anything like that. He usually couldn't get enough of her.

*What a time to disappear . . .*

"Well if it ain't the blushing bride-to-be." Viola Rose came up to greet us, menus in hand. "That wedding day'll be here before you know it."

"Viola Rose, you don't see one person standing here blushing," Miss Vivee said. "We just came for a meal."

"And who ya'll got wit'cha?" she said ignoring Miss Vivee. "Can't say I've seen hind nor hair of the two of you before." Viola Rose looked at my family.

"This is my mother, Justin, and my brother, Micah," I said.

"That's *Doctor* Justin Dickerson," Miss Vivee said. "She's a famous archaeologist. And her brother, Micah is a lawyer. So you better watch your step now that he's gonna be family. I got him on retainer." She punched a finger toward Micah, who just chuckled.

*She'd never pointed out that I had "Doctor" in front of my name,* I thought. *She just seems overjoyed with my mother.*

"And Justin," Miss Vivee continued, "this is Viola Rose, Proprietor, along with her husband, Gus," she nodded toward the grill.

"You forgot to say home of the best egg salad this side of the Mississippi," Viola Rose said and poked me with her elbow.

"I didn't forget to say it," Miss Vivee said. "I just don't like to lie."

Viola Rose sucked her tongue. "Well, anyhoo. Welcome to Jellybean's or rather the Bat Cave for the two of them." She pointed at me and Miss Vivee. "They come here to do their crime solving."

"We do no such thing," Miss Vivee said.

1

My mother looked at Miss Vivee then at me. She seemed surprised that Miss Vivee said she didn't lie, when she'd been telling them since we'd gone to Seppie Love's house, and now giving conflicting stories on what we do at Jellybean's. I, on the other hand, didn't bat an eye, I was used to Miss Vivee's untruths.

"Okay. Now ya'll follow me," Viola Rose said. "I got Miss Vivee's favorite bench waitin' and ready. I knew it wouldn't be long before ya'll got here."

Once we were seated, menus passed out, Miss Vivee put her bag on the table and leaned over to my mother, who she insisted sit next to her. She whispered, "I don't have a favorite bench."

"I heard that," Viola Rose said and shook her head. "How ya'll put up with the likes of this one is a wonder to me."

"Watch your mouth there, Viola. I am still very much your elder."

"Don't I know it," Viola Rose said and winked at me. "I'll give ya'll a minute to look over the menus, meanwhile I'll get ya'll a little something to wet your whistle."

"Justin and I will have sweet tea," Miss Vivee said.

I looked at my mother, waiting for her to object. She wasn't big on anything sweet, and Pepsi was her drug of choice.

She didn't say a word.

"I'm not sure what Logan wants to drink," Miss Vivee said. "She's so fickle."

I let out a snort. "I'll have a Pepsi, Viola Rose," I said. "Just like I always do."

"And what about you young man?"

"I'll have water for right now," Micah said.

"Not much of an eater?" Viola Rose asked and touched Micah's shoulder.

"Don't worry," I said. "This one will be sure to eat. He'll eat anything and everything in his path."

"Well then watch out!" Viola Rose said. "'Cuz we got a lot of food here."

"So how do we go about finding the murderer?" my mother asked Miss Vivee after Viola Rose left. She seemed genuinely interested, wanting to jump right in.

"Cause of death first," Miss Vivee said.

"We have that," my mother said. "She was stung by an Asian Hornet."

"How did you know that, Ma?" Micah said looking up from studying his menu. "All you did was look at her."

"It's a talent that not many possess," Miss Vivee said matter-of-factly. "But some of us know just by looking."

*I'm guessing she figures Micah and I don't have that gift.*

"It was the holes in her arm," my mother said. "I've seen that before." She was quiet for a moment.

1

"The question is," she turned toward Miss Vivee. "How did an Asian hornet get to Yasamee, Georgia?"

"That is the question, Justin." Miss Vivee nodded. "And my answer is the killer brought it here."

Viola Rose came back with our drinks. She pulled a pen from behind her ear, and reached in a deep pocket of her black apron for an order pad.

"Ya'll ready to order," she asked, pen hovering over pad.

"Justin and I will have egg salad sandwiches," Miss Vivee said. "Now mind you, Justin," she turned and looked at my mother, "I've had better, but it is worth trying." Miss Vivee handed her menu to Viola Rose, who just shook her head.

My mother didn't say a word about Miss Vivee ordering for her. She turned in her menu as well.

Micah didn't wait for Viola Rose to ask his order. "I'll have a double cheeseburger with bacon and the works," Micah spoke up. "French fries and a chocolate shake. And for an appetizer, I think I'll have this Chicken-in-a-Basket. Those are wings, right?"

"Sure are," Viola Rose said. "Anything else?" she asked eyebrow raised.

"Just a Pepsi, but you can bring that with my meal," he said. "Oh, and a salad with ranch dressing. Extra ranch."

"I see you were right about your brother, Logan." Viola Rose chuckled.

"Told you," I said.

"She knows me well," Micah said and bumped my shoulder with his.

"And what about you, Logan? Wha'cha having?"

"The same as my brother," I said. "Minus the Chicken-in-a-Basket, chocolate shake, and salad."

"Okay, it'll be right up." Viola Rose looked at Miss Vivee. "Where's Mac? He MIA?"

"He's minding his business, Viola Rose, just like you should be," Miss Vivee said.

"Well, it just seemed to me that with the latest murder victim still fresh at the morgue you'd three would have your thinking caps on. She was a wild child, no doubt. Gallivanting all over the world, dropping out of college, no money of her own to speak of, and spending her daddy's money like it was water. She probably had made a lot of enemies, even her best friend, and her cheating ex-boyfriend might be on your list of suspects. But she didn't deserve to die, and it'd be nice to solve it before the wedding."

"I don't have a list," Miss Vivee said and pulled the plastic bag with her notepad in it off the table and onto her seat. "And if I did, I wouldn't need your help putting names on it."

"I'm just saying," Viola Rose said holding up her hands like she was surrendering. "This one might be a hard one to solve. You'll probably need Mac."

"No harder than any of the others," Miss Vivee said.

Miss Vivee leaned over after Viola Rose had collected the rest of the menus and whispered, "That's

1

why you have to be careful about what we tell her. She is the biggest gossiper this side of the Mississippi River."

I rolled my eyes. That was the reason that Miss Vivee came to Jellybean's. To get information from Viola Rose.

"So you think the killer brought the hornet here on purpose?" my mother said getting back to the conversation she and Miss Vivee were having before Viola Rose took our food orders.

"I think it was an accident," Micah said before Miss Vivee could speak. "It got into her luggage when she was in China and she brought it home."

"Her last stop was India," I said. "You're probably just thinking of that article I read to you off my laptop where all those people in China were stung."

"India. China. Wherever." He held out his hand. "I think that's what happened."

"Can it live that long?" I asked and reached for my phone.

"I got it," he said. "'Okay, Google,'" he spoke into his cell phone. "What is the life span of an Asian Hornet?"

Micah tapped on his phone a few times then took to reading to himself.

"Read it out loud," Miss Vivee said and reached across the table, waving her hand to get Micah's attention.

"Oh," he said and looked at me smiling. "Okay."

I had warned him, Miss Vivee could be a handful.

"'The average life span of hornets in the wild is several months,'" Micah read. "'The general saying, born in spring, lives until fall is applicable to most hornets.'" He looked up. "So technically, it could've lived in her suitcase, gotten tangled up in her clothes, and stung her when she put them on."

"Yeah, but Micah, didn't you say it was about 50mm long? That's about 2.2 inches," I said. "She would have noticed that thing buzzing in her carry-on."

"She might not have had a carry-on, she was gone a long time."

I whipped out my phone and did a Google search of my own. "Oh my goodness, Micah," I said. "Look how big these things are." I showed him a picture of a man with four on his hand. "They are the entire width of this guy's hand."

I showed my mother and Miss Vivee the picture.

"Yeah, Micah," my mother said. "They are pretty big. And they have an even longer wingspan."

"Seventy-six millimeters," I read from my phone. I looked at him. "That's nearly three inches."

"So you can convert from the metric system in your head, doesn't mean someone killed her. She'd been gone a long time, was someone just lying in wait with a giant hornet until she returned?"

I was familiar with that logic. I had used it on my mother and Miss Vivee earlier. I looked at Micah. It was rather disheartening that now I was thinking like

1

my brother. I scrolled down to finish reading the article.

"Oh my," I said. "I looked up and smiled and my mother and Miss Vivee. "Now I see how you knew," I said. I showed Micah the pictures that had come up on my phone. "Look at the holes that thing leaves."

There was a picture of a man that had been stung in his arm several times, the holes formed after the sting were scattered across his limb and looked like the size of bullet wounds.

Micah took my phone and I saw his lips moving as he read the caption of the picture. "So when an Asian hornet bites, it bores a hole?"

"Yes," my mother said and Miss Vivee nodded. "When it *stings*," she corrected.

"That's what I meant," he said.

"Let me see," my mother said wiping her hands on a napkin and reaching for the phone. Micah passed it across the table.

"I don't know," Micah said. "It's big, but still small enough to get tangled up in some clothes, or in a shoe, a cosmetic bag or something. It's not impossible."

"Improbable," I said.

"But not impossible," he repeated. "It could still be an accident. It lives long enough to have survived the trip. Even if she didn't get it at the last place. Heck, it could've been her first stop.

"I don't think so," I said.

Viola Rose interrupted with our supper. Micah's spread nearly covered the entire table.

"Mmmmm. This is good." Miss Vivee had taken a huge bite (huge for her) out of her egg salad sandwich. "You enjoying yours?" she asked my mother.

"Yummy," my mother said.

Miss Vivee had finally gotten someone to eat egg salad with her. She was always ordering it for me, but I'd never touch the stuff.

"I think someone may have killed her because of the relic," my mother said wiping her mouth with a napkin. She picked up the conversation giving her theory. She took a sip of the tea and frowned up, I knew it was too sweet for her.

"Oh Logan, there goes Mommy with her Dan Brown conspiracy theories," Micah said.

"Say what you will, Micah," my mother said. "But Logan and I both know, *firsthand*, what people will do to get their hands on, and gain any subsequent fame, from ancient artifacts. They will kill. Logan saw a man die right in front of her eyes. And you must have forgotten that I was kidnapped."

"I didn't forget," he said. "And I'm not making light of your . . . Uhm . . . What happened to you and Logan. And yes, it does happen – did happen – but to happen again?" He shook his head. "This isn't the movies."

"Well, I think it was a love triangle," Miss Vivee said. "And Seppie and Keith killed her."

1

"Miss Vivee," I said. "You always think it's a love triangle, and it hasn't been yet."

"That just means that it's time for my theory to be the right one."

"So if there really isn't an artifact, Micah, why the postcard?" my mother asked, she evidently wasn't ready to move past her theory. "There has to be something to it."

"Logan told me what that Seppie Love, or whatever her name is, said," Micah said. "Kimmie learned how to play practical jokes from her stepmom, Frankie. Isn't that right, Logan?" I nodded, then he pointed to Miss Vivee. "I believe Seppie said it right. Kimmie might have been upset about her friend and boyfriend hanging out. She wanted to play a trick on them, so she mailed the postcard."

"That doesn't even make sense, Micah," I said. "How does that get Seppie and Keith back for that? A revenge plan that only makes you laugh? It might be a practical joke, but not to retaliate against them."

"I dunno," Micah said and shrugged. "Maybe that was just part of the joke, and she didn't have time to let it play out because of her *accident*."

"It was murder," the three of us said nearly in unison.

Micah held up his hand in mock surrender. "Geesh," he said. "A guy can't have an opinion."

"Not when it's wrong," I said, a smirk on my face.

"So, how do we decide who's right, Miss Vivee?" my mother said.

"We have to investigate," Miss Vivee said and chewed on her bottom lip like she was thinking.

"What is there to investigate?" my mother asked.

I wasn't worried about Miss Vivee coming up with something, or someone to investigate. I was just worried that what she came up with might get us thrown in jail, or killed.

1

Chapter Fifteen

"How about a little dessert?" Miss Vivee said. "I have an idea of what we should do next. We can discuss it over some sweets and a cup of coffee."

"I'd like that," my mother said. "What's good here?"

"Not the peach cobbler, Mommy," I said. "Peach pits kill."

"*A lot* of peach pits kill," Miss Vivee said. "And there aren't any in the peach cobbler."

"I'm having some," Micah said.

"You're going to eat more?" Miss Vivee asked.

"Dessert, right?" Micah asked. "Dessert isn't extra, it goes with the meal."

"I would have hated to feed that one," Miss Vivee said.

"We still feed him," my mother said. "That's why my husband and I can't afford to retire."

We all laughed. Micah turned around and beckoned for Viola Rose.

I skipped desert. And while they ate theirs and sipped piping hot coffee, Miss Vivee pulled out her suspect notebook, and licked the tip of her No. 2 pencil.

"Suspects," she said as she scrawled on the page.

"We only have two names," my mother said.

"Wrong," Miss Vivee said. "We have three. September Love and Keith Collier," she wrote. "And Macomber Whitson." She finished with a flourish.

"And we have a John Doe suspect, or suspects," my mother said.

"Who?" I asked.

"Whoever chased Kimmie here and killed her for the artifact she claimed to possess."

"Mom," Micah said. He didn't want her to go down that path.

"It might even be a cadre of evil mercenaries, backed by Christian zealots with ties to the Vatican," my mother said, going down that road anyway.

"See," Micah said. "It *is* like Dan Brown."

"I'll just write 'Zealots,' Justin," Miss Vivee said and licked her pencil. "At least until we can find out their real names."

*I am not going to be able to take the both of them together for much longer.*

"So how will we find out?" my mother asked.

"We'll have to do a little B & E job."

Micah's fork stopped at the opening of his mouth. He dropped it onto his plate, mouth still wide. "'B & E' as in breaking and entering?"

"We can leave you out if you think it's a conflict of interest," Miss Vivee said.

1

"Mom?" Micah looked at her questioningly.

"Miss Vivee knows what she's doing," my mother said. "She's solved six murders already."

"Actually seven," Miss Vivee said and held her chin a little higher. Evidently proud of her accomplishment. "The seventh was a cold case." She nodded. "Sixty-six years old. I'll tell you about that one later."

"You're not going to break in somewhere are you?" he asked our mother. "Really, Mom?" He picked up his phone. "I'm calling Dad."

"Hold your horses," Miss Vivee said. "I was thinking we'd just have a looksee around Stallings Inn."

"Stallings Inn?" he asked as if the name sounded familiar.

"That's Frankie Hunt's place," I said. "You know, Kimmie's stepmom."

"I know who Frankie Hunt is," he said. "I've stayed in the same house with her since I got to Georgia."

"She gave us the key, Micah," my mother said. "Miss Vivee, you've got the key, right?"

"Sure do," Miss Vivee said and pulled out a set of keys. She jiggled them, making them clink.

I recognized them as the keys to Miss Vivee's car and the Maypop's four car garage.

"We can go and look through Kimmie's things. Under the bed, in the drawers," Miss Vivee said. "Maybe there's a clue there."

"You can't go and mess up that woman's house," Micah said.

"Hi," came a deep voice from behind me before anyone could address Micah's concerns.

*Bay.*

My heart almost stopped beating. Just the sound of his voice gave me goose pimples up and down my arms. I was too embarrassed to even try and relay how he made the rest of me feel.

I pushed down in my seat, and shifted, turning around to see him, his smell enveloping my senses.

I took in a nostril full and closed my eyes. Emanating from him was a citrusy scent of oranges and lemons mixed with wood, and jasmine.

And when I opened my eyes, they were met with his twinkling, hazel ones.

"Hello there," he said. He stood behind the bench looking down at me. A sexy smile on his face.

"Hi," I said breathily.

*Oh goodness.* I felt like I was in a cheap B movie. I cleared my throat.

"Hey, Bay." I tried to sound more normal. I glanced over at my mother, she was eating her peach cobbler, not paying any attention to me.

"So we heard that you might have to take over the investigation of Kimberly Hunt's murder," Miss Vivee said.

"Don't get any ideas, Grandmother," Bay said. "You and Logan don't have the time to get involved in this. I've talked to the Sheriff."

1

"That big mouth," Miss Vivee muttered.

"He's trying to do his job."

"I'm not interfering with his job," Miss Vivee said. "Although he isn't very good at it."

"Grandmother. Please. Just let the upcoming nuptials keep you two occupied." He winked at me. "Or maybe I should say, the three of you," Bay said and looked at my mother."

"I just asked if you were taking over the investigation," Miss Vivee said. "Don't go dragging our guest into your insinuations. And don't get all riled up about a little innocent question."

"Grandmother, there is nothing innocent about you," he said.

"Why thank you," Miss Vivee said and smiled. She wiped her mouth with her napkin. "I've worked long and hard to gain that reputation."

"You'd think you'd behave in front of company," he said.

"Justin and Micah aren't company, she said. They're family. Or will be."

Bay looked down at me and smiled. I blushed and lowered my head.

*Why am I so corny?*

"I came by to see if Micah wanted to go to the mall with me. I have to pick up my tux."

"Sure, Man. I'll go," Micah said. "Just let me finish up my cobbler."

"Cool," Bay said. "So what are you ladies up to after this? Going back home?"

I turned around and looked at my mother, she looked at me. No way could we tell Bay the plan we'd just concocted.

Micah didn't even lift his head up, he kept spooning cobbler into his mouth.

"We're just going and do a little pop-calling. You know," Miss Vivee said. "Be neighborly. One of our own has just died. Everyone needs a little comfort."

We looked at Miss Vivee and then at Bay.

*Was he going to believe that?*

"Oh good," he said and smiled. "It's kind of late, but I'm sure folks around here wouldn't mind company." He smiled. "I'm glad you came up with something like that to do. And I'm glad you're including Logan's family."

My mother and I looked at Miss Vivee. Her face hadn't changed. She wasn't giving away anything.

"Well, my word, Bay, why wouldn't I include them?" Miss Vivee said. "You talk as if I wouldn't know how to entertain them. What did you think? I take them out on a home invasion, and we'd ransack a house?"

Micah choked on his cobbler. He put a napkin up to his mouth to keep it from spewing across the table. My mother turned and looked out of the window, and I just tucked my head.

1

Chapter Sixteen

Micah went with Bay to Augusta. He didn't complain one iota, even though according to him he didn't want to be bothered with any wedding preparation stuff.

Meanwhile, my mother, Miss Vivee and I prepared to burglarize Stallings Inn.

Miss Vivee insisted that I check Hadley's Drugstore to see if they'd gotten any ski masks in. When I reminded her they didn't have any the last time she wanted us to break into a private residence, she informed me she'd subsequently called and placed a special order for them.

*I should've known.*

Miss Vivee and my mother waited in the car while I went into Hadley's to purchase the masks. They had two black ones, and a red one, the crown covered in white diamond shapes with green and blue dots inside.

I climbed back in the car and as soon as I pulled the door shut, Miss Vivee had her hand out. "Well, let's see what you got."

I handed her one of the light blue plastic bags I gotten from Hadley's.

"Whoever heard of selling a red and white ski mask?" Miss Vivee asked pulling it out of the bag and examining it.

"I don't think they knew you wanted to use it for illegal activities," I said.

"Why else would I want a ski mask in the middle of summer?" she said. "I declare. Some people just ain't got the good sense God gave 'em."

I just shook my head.

"Did you get the flashlights," she asked.

"Yes," I said. I pulled out one from the other bag.

"Those are awfully big," she said and reached for one.

"They're normal sized," I said pulling another one out. I turned it around in my hand, scrutinizing it.

"They don't fit," she said.

"Fit what?"

I looked over at her and she had her mouth opened in the shape of an "O" and was trying to stick the end of the flashlight in.

"Miss Vivee," I said and took it from her. "What are you doing?"

"You're supposed to hold it in your mouth so your hands are free to do things."

I closed my eyes and took in a breath. Opening them, I glanced in the mirror and saw that my mother had fallen over on the seat laughing.

1

"You're not going to open a safe, Miss Vivee," I said.

"You don't know that for sure," she said.

*I knew this was a bad idea.*

"Give me this stuff," I said and gathered up the hats and flashlights. I leaned over, popped opened the glove compartment and threw them inside. "We don't need any of those things, Miss Vivee. We're just going over there to check out the place, make sure it's ready for the overflow from the Maypop."

"No we're not," Miss Vivee said and frowned up.

"That's our cover, Miss Vivee," my mother said. "In case anyone sees us."

Miss Vivee looked at me. "Is that what you meant?"

"Yes. Frankie did give us the key-"

"I don-"

"Uuh. Uuh," I held up my hand. "I already know you don't have the key. I saw the ones you showed Micah."

"So you know we're going to have to break in?"

"I know that we're going to have to be *creative* about getting in, yes."

Miss Vivee smiled. She turned her head, straining to look in the backseat at my mother. "Justin, your daughter's using her noggin. Today."

I looked in the rearview mirror and saw my mother shaking her head still laughing.

I drove over to Stallings Inn and the whole house was dark.

"Maybe I should park down the street," I said.

"I thought we were just checking on it for the extra guests?" Miss Vivee said.

"That's if we get caught once we're inside," I said. "How can we justify that story if they see us prying a lock open?"

"How am I supposed to know?" Miss Vivee said. "It was your idea."

"Where's Mr. Hunt?" my mother asked.

"Remember Frankie said he had camped out at the Sheriff's office?"

"I know," my mother said. "But I figured that with him being sick and all, he might come home at night."

"What's wrong with him?" I asked.

"I don't know," Miss Vivee said. "And we don't know if we can trust that Seppie Love either. Frankie said he wasn't sick. But I know how we can find out." She reached for the door handle.

I parked a couple houses down from Stallings Inn. We grabbed the flashlights I'd purchased at Hadley's and walked to the house.

Standing in front of it, I stared at it through the darkness. The front lit only by a gas light in the yard and a street light on the other side of the street. "Should I go around back and see if I can get in the kitchen window?" I asked

"I think we should try the front door first," Miss Vivee said. "A lot of people still don't lock their doors."

"Okay," I said. "I'll go and see. Stay put."

1

I ran up on the porch and tried the door. It was locked. I thought about going around back, but decided to first check one of the windows that lined the porch. And, yay! I found one. Shoving it up, I put one foot in, straddling I ducked my head in and pulled my other leg through.

"Come to the door," I said through the opened window. "I'll let you in."

Shutting the window back, I flipped on my flashlight and flashed a quick beam around the interior of the house, then over to the door. The inside floor of the door was scattered with mail. I shined a light on it – magazines, bills, an invoice – I looked at the return addresses and then noticed a couple that looked like greeting cards. Condolences for Kimmie, no doubt, but they couldn't have been mailed. She'd just died. I guessed they probably had just been pushed through the door.

I gingerly stepped over them as not to disturb the pile, and then thought how obvious we were being by "breaking in" through the front of the house. I opened the front door and let in my partners in crime.

"Watch the mail," I said. "Don't fall." I closed the door after they came in and shined my light up the stairs. They weren't as ornate or sturdy looking as the Maypop's.

"First thing we want to find is what's ailing Nash Hunt," Miss Vivee said.

"I agree," I said. "So we'll start upstairs," I said. "Where the bedrooms are." I headed up the creaky steps, but once I reached the top, I noticed Miss Vivee hadn't followed me.

"Miss Vivee," I whispered as loud as I could over the banister, back downstairs. "Miss Vivee!" I looked over at my mother and then shined the light back down stairs. "What are you doing?"

"Looking through the mail," she said. "Might be a clue."

"What? Why?" I ran back down the steps. She had the mail in her hand. I took it from her and dropped it back on the floor, trying to make it look as if it fell from the chute.

"We might find something," she repeated.

"I don't think whoever killed Kimmie wrote a letter and sent it to her parents' home."

"Well, what about Nash?" she said as I pushed her toward the steps. "We need to find out about him."

"The only way you could find out anything about him, would be to *open* the mail. We're not disturbing anything. Plus, I looked at the return addresses on some of them. Nothing medical."

"Are you sure?"

"I'm sure," I said. "Let's go upstairs."

Once upstairs, Miss Vivee went straight to the medicine cabinet in the first bathroom we got to. "Nothing's here," she said.

"People only keep medicine in the bathroom cabinet in the movies," I said. My mother and I was standing in the doorway.

1

"They do not," Miss Vivee wrinkled her forehead, adding more lines to the plethora of them already there. "Why would they call it a medicine chest if it wasn't for that?"

"Let's try a nightstand," I suggested. "Look for a bedroom." We were in the middle of a burglary. We didn't have time to argue.

We found our way into Frankie's bedroom, and discovered there wasn't anything in it that belonged to Mr. Hunt.

"You think she makes him sleep on the couch?" Miss Vivee asked. "She's such a mean thing. Him sick and all."

"We don't know for sure that he's sick," I said. "And maybe he's the mean one."

"You'll be married soon, you'll see how women give grief for no good reason. Some of them are rascals, no doubt, but most of them just don't have good sense. That's why they act like they do. We just have to tolerate their dumbness better. That's how you be a good wife. Ask your mother." She pointed to my mom.

"I'm not in this one," she said and looked at me. "But you lived with your father and brother, you should be able to figure out that one yourself."

I closed my eyes and shook my head. I didn't know how my mother could agree with anything Miss Vivee said.

"How about if we keep looking?" my mother said. "Maybe this Nash Hunt had a bedroom all his own."

We went down the hallway, opening each, flashing a light to look around. Not one looked occupied.

"How about downstairs?" my mother suggested. "Your house has a bedroom downstairs, maybe this one does, too."

"Of course it does," Miss Vivee said. "But I still think she would stick him on the couch."

I lead the way down the back stairs, holding the flashlight up like a torch. We found an in-law suite off the kitchen and down a short corridor.

"This one smells like a nest of granddaddies," Miss Vivee said after I opened the door. "I betcha this is where he sleeps."

My mother laughed, but I knew just what Miss Vivee meant. The room reeked of stale cigarettes and dirty socks.

All of us focused our beams in the room. It was sparsely furnished. A full-sized bed was in the middle of the floor, neatly made. A chest of drawers, a chair, and a nightstand with a lamp and a clock atop of it was all there was. The room was dark – the shades were drawn, and it was warmer than the other rooms in the house. Off the bedroom was a small bathroom.

"In there," Miss Vivee said. She pointed to the bathroom with the beam from her flashlight. I guess it was her medicine cabinet idea again.

I went to the nightstand, turned on the lamp and pulled opened the small drawer. I found it full of pill

1

bottles. I st on the side of the bed and pulled each one out one-by-one.

The bottles were all from pharmacies located in a place called Baxley, Georgia. Most of them from Barnes Pharmacy that had an address on Main Street.

"Miss Vivee," I yelled over my shoulder. "Where is Baxley, Georgia?"

"A couple hours south of here, not too far from Savannah. Why?" she said coming out from the bathroom.

I turned around on the bed. "What were you two doing in there so long? Did you find something?"

"Some shaving cream," Miss Vivee said and tossed it on the bed.

"What did you find?" my mother said. She came to sit next to me on the bed.

"A lot of pills." I pointed to the opened nightstand drawer.

"Let me see," my mother said and took the bottles from my hand. "Adriamycin," she read the label.

"That sounds like an antibiotic," I said.

"Avastin. Plantinol." She kept reading.

"I know that one," Miss Vivee said. "That Plantinol. Louis took it."

"Bay's father?" I asked.

"How many other Louis's do you know?"

I hadn't known him, but there was one thing I did know about him. "Bay's father had cancer," I said, sharing what I knew with my mother. "Maybe Mr. Hunt does too?"

I pulled out my phone and Googled the last name my mother read out. "'Plantinol.'" I read. "'Brand name for the drug, Cisplatin. It is an anti-cancer medication that interferes with the growth of cancer cells and slows their growth and spread in the body. The drug is used to treat testicular, ovarian, bladder, head and neck, esophageal, small and non-small cell lung, breast, cervical, stomach and prostate cancers.'" I looked at my mother.

"Well that narrows it down," she said.

I shrugged. "So, we still don't know exactly what's wrong with him," I said.

"We know he's got cancer, and that ain't good," Miss Vivee said.

"I'll call Claire," my mother said. "Give me your phone. I'm sure she'll know."

My mother's sister, Claire, had four degrees, including a medical one. She didn't practice, instead she ran a research lab at the Cleveland Clinic. It didn't take long for her to narrow down what Mr. Hunt was suffering from once my mother read all the labels in the drawer.

"Lung cancer," my mother announced after she ended the call with her sister. "Claire's says she's 99% positive. She said she would be 100% sure, but it wouldn't be good to make such a determination without ever having seen him."

"Lung cancer. That's curable nowadays," Miss Vivee said and opened up one of the bottle of pills. "But it sure doesn't make him 'healthy as a horse' like

1

Frankie said." She held up one of the pills. "Although this pill is big enough for a horse." She screwed the lid back on and tossed it in the drawer.

"I don't think he could be 'frisky as a fritter,' either," I said.

"Ferret," my mother said. "Frankie said he was 'frisky as a ferret.'" She looked at me, then Miss Vivee. "Claire said with the combination of medication he's taking, it sounds like he might be Stage IV."

"Oh," Miss Vivee said and nothing else.

"Fritter. Ferret. Whatever," I said. "Frankie wasn't telling the truth if Auntie Claire is right. And I believe her. Mr. Hunt is very sick."

Miss Vivee shook her head. "That's *gawd* awful! He's got to suffer like that and then lose his only child, all at the same time."

"Now that we know what ails Mr. Hunt," I said. "Let's see if we can find out what Miss Kimmie had been up to that may have gotten her killed." I looked at my mother and then nodded toward the hallway. "Her bedroom must be down here, too."

We found two other doors down the narrow hallway, one was a bathroom, and the other was the room we were looking for.

Opening the door to Kimmie's room should have triggered a parting of the clouds and an angelic choral refrain. The room was beautiful and looked nothing like the rest of the house. It had sky blue walls with sheer curtains, that matched exactly, hanging ceiling to floor. Everything else was white and golden. The brass bed was shiny, and the light of the glass chandelier glinted off of it and made it gleam. A fluffy, cloud-like, comforter and pillows covered the bed which set on a soft, short shaggy rug. Everything was neatly in place, and looked more like a layout for a magazine than an actual living space.

"Where to start?" I said standing at the door, darting a beam of light around the room, and staring in.

"The drawers," Miss Vivee said squeezing past me.

"I'll check the closet," my mother said walking over. She swung the door open. "This is kind of creepy," she said. "Going through a dead person's things."

"Isn't that what you do for a living?" Miss Vivee said.

I grimaced. I certainly agreed with what my mother said. Archaeologist didn't deal with the newly departed.

I walked over to Kimmie's dresser and found a small, flip photo album sitting near the edge. I slowly turned the pages and found picture after picture of Kimmie. She had been a beautiful girl. Dark, silky hair, olive-colored skin, and blue eyes the color of her walls. And to my surprise, the little book was filled with photos of Keith Collier, the man we'd seen at Seppie Love's house half dressed. The pictures were evidence that Kimmie and Keith had been an item –

1

the loving stares and cuddling in nearly every one –
showed much more than a friendship. And Seppie
Love was not in one of them. That raised questions
about what September and Keith were up to now.

"Here's something to look through," my mother
said breaking my chain of thought. She pulled a duffle
bag from the closet floor. It still had airline tags on it.

"What you got?" Miss Vivee asked pushing the
last drawer shut. "Because I didn't find anything
there."

"Her luggage," my mother said. "If she's got some
kind of ancient artifact from her travels, she may have
it in here."

"Not a very good hiding place," Miss Vivee said.
"That'd be the first place for anyone to look."

My mother unzipped the bag without
commenting. We all leaned over and peered inside. It
was full of clothes and shoes, and was packed just as
neatly as her room looked.

"Let's see if there are any hidden compartments,"
my mother said and started to run her hand around the
interior when we heard footsteps.

I flicked my flashlight off, and my mother
followed suit. Miss Vivee flickered hers in my face.

"What was that?" she asked in a normal voice.

"Shh!" I said. I took the flashlight from her and
turned it off. "Hold on." I walked over to the window
and peeked out.

"What do you see?" Miss Vivee asked.

"Nothing," I said turning to them. I could only see an outline of the two, standing over the bed, my mother's silhouette showing she was still clutching onto the bag. I walked over to the door, closed it and turned my flashlight back on. Focusing the beam toward the floor, I instructed my mother to put the bag back.

"We need to go," I said.

She zipped it up, and after guiding her back to the closet, I shut off the light, slowly opened the door and taking in a breath, I peered around the corner.

"C'mon," I said, unsure if they could see me waving them on. Then we heard footsteps overhead. I quickly closed the door back. "Crap!"

"They're upstairs," Miss Vivee said.

"I know," I said. "I hear them."

"I mean, they are upstairs," she said again.

"So what she means is, we can go," my mother said.

"Right," I said nodding my head. I opened the door again. "Maybe we should go out the back door." It was more of statement than a request for approval.

"We are the proprietors of Stallings Inn," Miss Vivee said.

"What?" I said in a strained whisper.

"By proxy," she said her voice getting louder, she stomped her foot, "maybe we should go and see who's up there."

I was tempted to throw her five-foot nothing, ninety-something frame over my shoulder and carry

1

her out, instead I gave her arm a little tug, and in a not so nice, but very firm voice said, "Let's go."

But still, she didn't seem to understand the urgency.

"That's Frankie's so-called greenhouse," Miss Vivee said once we were out back. "I want to check it out, see what she has."

I looked over at the crooked shack, and couldn't believe she wanted to take time to look in it. "I don't think that's a greenhouse, Miss Vivee. It has all of two windows," I whispered, but I'm sure she heard the stress in my voice. "And we have to go."

"Just a little peek," she said walking toward it.

I grabbed her arm with one hand, and put my other arm around her shoulder. "We have to go. Now!"

"Close call," my mother said as I pulled the car up into the driveway of the Maypop. I didn't pull all the way in, so I could help my elderly cohorts out of the car closer to the front door.

"I know," I said and eyed Miss Vivee.

"Oh good heavens," Miss Vivee said. "I thought we were Frankie's proxy. What happened to that alibi?"

*I must not be living right if I need an alibi . . .*

"It was just something I said, in case we got caught."

"Exactly," Miss Vivee said. "So if they had of caught us, then that's what we would have told them."

"And why would we tell them we were using flashlights?" I asked.

"Flashlights were your idea," Miss Vivee said.

*I guess she forgot she's the one who made me buy them.*

"But who is *they*?" my mother asked. "Unless Renmar did rent out a room, no one should have been there."

"If we had of stayed, we could have found out," Miss Vivee said. "It might have been whoever killed Kimmie."

"Then we'd be dead, just like Kimmie."

Miss Vivee waved her hand, dismissing me. "I'm sure it was just guests, wouldn't you say, Justin?"

"Probably," my mother agreed.

"We'll ask Renmar," Miss Vivee said. "Well looka there." Miss Vivee pointed out the window at an older man coming down the front steps of the Maypop. "That's Nash Hunt." She rolled down her window. "Stay put. I want to talk to him."

"Don't tell him we were just at his house," I said concern in my voice "Remember, it was a covert operation."

"Don't I know it. Couldn't even look in the shed," she said waving me off. "Blow the horn."

I blew it, and then she called out "Yoohoo! Nash!" She reached over and blew the horn again.

"He's coming," I said.

1

Mr. Hunt smiled, waved, and ambled his way over to the car. I watched him as slowly made his way, he wore a baseball cap, blue jeans, and a plaid shirt that he was tucked tightly into his pants. He seemed to have a hard time breathing, his chest heaving up and down, his mouth slightly opened like he was sucking in extra air. He came around the car and leaned in, arms folded across the opened window.

He touched the brim of his hat. "Evening ladies," then smiled at Miss Vivee. "Kind of late for you to be out, ain't it?" he said.

"I did my time inside, Nash," Miss Vivee said. "Logan came and broke me out." She patted his hand. "Our condolences to you."

"Thank you," he said.

Miss Vivee pointed to me. "This is Bay's fiancé, Logan, and her mother, Dr. Justin Dickerson."

"Hi," my mother and I chimed in, both trying to sound chipper.

"Hello," he said and gave us a weak smile.

"I heard that Kimmie came back home just to see you, Nash," Miss Vivee said.

"She lived here, she didn't need to come visit," he said.

"I also heard that you ain't been feeling so well."

"I'm doing good," he said and glanced back over to the house. "Can't believe much that Francesca says." He coughed into his balled fist. "I'll be hitting seventy-three come this November, so, for an old man, I'm doing just fine."

"Do tell," Miss Vivee said and smiled. "Especially one with a young wife to keep up with."

Miss Vivee spoke like Frankie was a spring chicken, she may have been younger than he was, but I knew she was at least as old as my mother. And to me, that was old.

Mr. Hunt licked his lips and took a more serious tone. "But you know, Miss Vivee," he lowered his voice. "I've been going down to Baxley to see a doctor. And what they're thinkin' ain't so good. I had even made arrangements already to leave everything to Kimmie once I was gone so she could continue on her travels." He smiled. "She loved it so much."

"Everything to Kimmie?" Miss Vivee asked.

"Well, of course I'd see to Frankie havin' what she needed if'n something happened to me. But Kimmie was my baby girl."

"Now you're making arrangements for her, huh?"

He hung his head. "It's breaking my heart."

"I know it is," Miss Vivee said.

"Now, I can't just give in, you know? I can't leave this earth 'til I find out what happened to her." He sucked in a gulp of air. "I was wondering. Do you think you got something 'round back in that greenhouse of yours that could help me out?"

Miss Vivee placed her hand on his arm, and smiled a warm smile. "You stop on around, Nash. And we'll see what we can do."

"Alright then. I appreciate it." He tipped his hat and stepped away from the car. "Ladies," he said.

1

"And don't you worry none, I'll wait until after the wedding, Miss Vivee, then I'll come 'round."

"You're welcomed anytime, Nash."

"Miss Vivee," my mother said as Mr. Hunt walked away. "You know there isn't a cure for cancer."

"I know that," Miss Vivee said. "But there's a cure for the hurt and despair that comes along with it. It's called hope." Miss Vivee nodded her head. "And that's what I plan on giving him. A little hope."

Chapter Seventeen
Friday, 8:30am

*Two days before the wedding . . .*

"My house has been ransacked!"
The three of us looked at each other.
"What kind of people are you sending to my bed and breakfast?" Frankie was up in Renmar's face. But Renmar stood firm, not even flinching, while Frankie's arms were flailing and spit spewed from her mouth. "It'll take me months to clean up that place for it to be decent enough for guests." She wagged her finger in Renmar's face. "Are you prepared to offer me compensation?"
Miss Vivee leaned in, "We didn't ransack that place," she whispered. "We hardly touched anything."
"I know," I said and leaned in, pulling my mother close. "What is she talking about?"
"I don't know, but it must have been the noise we heard," Miss Vivee whispered.
"*Noise* can't ransack a house," I whispered back.

1

"But the people who made the noise could," she said. "Don't get smart with me."

"I thought we decided it was just one of the guests," my mother lowered her voice.

"Miss Vivee was going to ask Renmar if she'd rented a room out." I looked at her. "Did you ask her?"

"And when would I have had time? We were out on the case all day yesterday."

"A guest wouldn't ransack the place," my mother said.

"No they wouldn't. So, I'm beginning to think that maybe it wasn't a guest who came in," Miss Vivee said. "I'm thinking it might have been our 'Artifact Hunters.'"

"Artifact hunters?" I said face frowned up. "What are you talking about?"

"Mother," Renmar interjected into our conversation from across the room. She pushed past Frankie, who let out a big huff. "What do you three have your heads together about?" she asked. "Do you all know something about this?"

My mother and I sprung up and sat straight.

"Of course we don't," Miss Vivee said. "We were just talking about what a terrible thing to happen to Frankie. That's all. And, we three agreed that we'd volunteer to clean it up."

I tried not to give away our real conversation, but my face must have shown that what Miss Vivee had said wasn't the truth.

"What are you three really up to, Logan?" Renmar said, eyeing me. "Did ya'll have something to do with this?"

*Why does she always call me out?*

"Uh-uh." I shook my head. I was afraid to say anything else.

My mother elbowed me, then cleared her throat. "Of course she doesn't know anything, but she was concerned that if someone would do that there, they might do it here, too. Right?"

I nodded.

"I think it's a good idea that we go over and clean up. Wouldn't you say, 'It's neighborly?'" my mother asked.

I didn't know what she was doing, but evidently she was in with Miss Vivee.

*Hadn't she had enough of illegal activities?*

"Well, that's nice of you three," Renmar said hesitantly. She turned and looked at Frankie, whose demeanor had changed, she now seemed flabbergasted.

"What's wrong, Frankie?" Miss Vivee said. "Cat got your tongue?"

"No," she eked out. "I just don't think it's necessary for you three to go and clean up." She swallowed hard. "It's . . . It's just that it's Renmar that's responsible. Plus, I don't know if it's a good thing for any of us to go in there."

"You heard Justin," Miss Vivee said. "It's the neighborly thing to do. And we *are* neighbors."

1

"Well, I was thinking that Bay or the Sheriff should go. First. I mean," Frankie said. "I don't know if someone is still in there or not."

"What was taken?" Miss Vivee asked.

"I don't know," she said and looked at us. "I was scared to look around. But it was mostly stuff in Kimmie's room that was amiss."

"I'll call the Sheriff," Renmar said. "That sounds like the right thing to do." She looked at us, and back at Frankie. "You come with me. I'm sure the Sheriff will want to hear from you about what happened.

"Why did you volunteer us to clean up?" I asked Miss Vivee.

"So we could look for clues."

"Didn't you stop to think that there wouldn't be any clues left after the Sheriff searched the place? He'd find them."

"No," she said. "I hadn't thought of that. But he doesn't know how to look for things like I do."

"He does, Miss Vivee," I said. "He's good at what he does, if you just give him a chance. Now we're stuck cleaning the place for no reason."

Chapter Eighteen

Sheriff Lloyd Haynes agreed to meet Frankie at her house to file a police report. He wanted Bay to come, but Bay denied jurisdiction, so he took newly deputized Junior Appletree and Mr. Hunt.

Nash Hunt looked different from when I'd seen him just the night before. Maybe it was the light of day, but he appeared frailer, and coughed much more. But the determination I saw in his eyes were palpable. He was determined to do whatever it took to help with finding out what happened to his daughter.

I still saw no reason to go there, especially if it involved me cleaning anything since we'd taken a look the night before – not a very good look – but a look nonetheless, and one thing we'd found out was there wasn't anything to see.

While we waited for the Sheriff to meet with Frankie, Bay, Micah, and I decided to go and see about Mac. I packed up some dessert for him.

I hadn't seen Mac since the morning of the murder, and I was getting worried about him. I was

1

even a little panicky that maybe he wouldn't show up to the wedding.

My mother stayed with Miss Vivee. They had decided to go over their suspect list. All three names. Oh, yeah, I forgot the unnamed "Zealots." None of which I agreed with. Well, I wasn't really sure I disagreed with Keith Collier. Did he and September really have something going and Kimmie found out?

Still, I hadn't had any "vibes" about anyone. Yet.

And, I had begun to believe that unlike all our other investigations, this one wasn't going to be solved quickly. So I had spoken to Marge, the wedding planner, at length. She assured me that if murder wasn't solved, the yellow caution tape wouldn't have to be worked into the design. She did have a contingency plan.

We had hired her so none of us would freak out or panic when problems arose, so I had decided to let her do her job. My job, at this point, was just to show up.

"Did you call Mac and let him know we were coming?" Bay asked as we headed out to his house.

"No," I said. "Miss Vivee never calls."

"You're not Miss Vivee," Bay said.

"I think it'll be okay."

I was hoping it would be as we walked up the steps to his house and rang the bell. With his moodiness of late, he may not welcome unexpected guests.

I heard him coming. The clump of his cane, the click of the heel of his one shoe, and the shuffle sound he made with his bad leg. And then the clinking of nails over the wood floor – Rover, his dog, was right behind him.

Mac peeked through the curtain and smiled at us. "Well, hello," he said pulling the door open wide. "What a welcomed surprise." Rover gave us a bark hello.

"I've missed you, Mac," I said. I bent down and gave Rover a scratch behind the ear.

"Have you now," he said and patted me on my shoulder. "And who is this fine young man?" he asked.

"That's my brother, Micah."

"The lawyer."

"Yes, sir," Micah said. "The lawyer." He chuckled.

"I brought you this," I said and handed him the brown paper bag with the desserts. "For your sweet tooth."

"I lost all those kinds of teeth years ago," Mac said. "But the ones I bought do appreciate the gesture."

"Wow. You have a lot of books," Micah said wandering into the front room.

"Only way to keep up with what's goings on in the world. I don't have one of those fancy phones like your sister. She gaggles everything."

"Gaggle?" Micah seemed amused.

"Google," I said. "And, Mac, I don't know how you can stuff more knowledge in that head of yours. You and Miss Vivee know everything."

1

"A jack of all trades, a master of none," he said.

Bay laughed. "I wouldn't sell yourself short. If my grandmother likes you, you couldn't be too bad."

"Well, I'm hoping to keep her interested." He gave Bay a faint smile. "Have a seat," Mac said. "Push a book out of the way if you have to. I'm going to take this in the kitchen. Anyone want anything to drink?"

"No," we all said.

"Well, I was thinking of sharing whatever goodies Logan brought me," he shook the brown bag, "with everyone."

"Well then, I'll take a glass of milk," Bay said. He snapped his finger calling Rover over to him.

"Bay," I said.

"Me too," Micah said. "I'll take a glass to go with a slice of that 7-Up cake."

"Oh my goodness," I said. I shouldn't have ever let them see what I'd packed. "I brought the desserts for Mac."

"I wouldn't feel right not sharing," Mac said.

"Well, I don't want anything," I said. "You share if you want to, but I wanted you to have it."

"Thank you little lady," Mac said and bowed. "Now you just talk amongst yourselves and I'll be right back."

I picked up a magazine that laid open on a plaid green armchair to move it out of my way, and plopped down in it. I started to close the magazine, but noticed the article it was opened to. It was entitled: *Hot Bee Balls Cook Enemy Hornets*.

"What is this?" I said not really loud enough for Mac to hear me. I started reading the article. The subtitle read: *In a battle with Asian giant hornets, Japanese honeybees turn up the heat – quite literally – by swarming around the hornets and cooking them to death.*

*What the hey . . .*

I finished reading the article, flipped it to the front to see the name of the periodical – hmmm, *National Geographic* – then flipped it back to the article and read it again.

"Bay," I said after I'd read through a second time, interrupting he and Micah's conversation. "Listen to this."

"What is it, Babe?" he said leaning forward on the couch.

"Remember all those bees at the crime scene?" I held out the magazine to him.

"No," he said. "I wasn't there, remember?"

"Oh yeah," I said.

"I remember," Micah said. "Well at least I remember the one. Scared the heck outta me."

Bay chuckled. "You scared of a bee, Man?"

"Heck yeah," Micah said.

"What you got?" Bay turned back to me, and nodded toward the magazine.

"This article says that honeybees have a defense mechanism that it uses to kill giant Asian hornets."

"What?" Micah said. "Bees killing those big hornets?"

1

"So?" Bay said looking at Micah then me. "What does it have to do with anything?"

"I dunno," I said. "But doesn't it seem a little coincidental that both the bees and hornets were in the same place? I mean, I've been going to the gazebo a few times a day to check on things, I never remember seeing a bee."

"Didn't Miss Vivee say that maybe it was because of the flowers she had planted?" Micah said.

"Yeah, at the crime scene. When we had stopped." I nodded my head. "I remember that, but it could've been put there to get rid of the hornets."

"How many hornets were there?" Micah asked.

"Not sure," I said. "It only takes one to kill a person."

"I don't think it's strange for both to be there," Bay said. "If bees have a built in defense mechanism against hornets, it's because they encounter them often. So they are usually in the same place."

"Listen to this," I said, thinking I might have a possible connection. I read from the article. "'The bees' strange defensive tactic evolved because their venomous stingers are too small to pierce the thick exoskeletons of the giant hornets—insects which can grow about two inches (five centimeters) long. The quivering of muscle fibers from so many bees creates real heat that kills off the predators.'"

"So sorry that it took me so long," Mac interrupted coming out of the kitchen with a tray filled with the desserts I had brought him. I didn't get to the part I wanted them to hear. "My neighbor came to the back door and no matter how many times I told her I had company, she kept saying she just had one more thing to tell me."

"That's okay, Mac," I said. "I found-"

"Well, really, it's not okay," he said. "When she finally got around to telling me what she wanted, I realized that she's got kind of an emergency. Her elderly mother is ill. She thought it was nothing, but I think I should have a look. The sooner, the better."

*Did he say "elderly?" I wonder doesn't he know that's what he is.*

"It's fine, Mac," Bay said. "We can go."

"No. No," Mac said. "I won't hear of it, at least not until you've had the cake and milk I poured for you. 'Waste not want not,' my father used to always say."

"That's not necessary, Mac," I said. I held up the magazine. "But I did want to -"

"I insist," he said cutting me off. "And who knows, maybe I'll make it back before you leave."

"Mac!" I said rather overzealously. "Wait!" I need to ask you about the bees." I shook the magazine.

"Oh isn't that a good article," he said. "And so relevant after Junior Appletree, or I should say *Deputy* Appletree, found that hive."

"What hive?" I asked.

"Over at the crime scene. Tree not too far from where Kimmie was found. None of us could

1

remember seeing it there before, but you know . . ." he smiled. "Could be a clue.

I looked at Bay. "A clue, huh?"

"Gotta go," Mac said.

We watched as Mac grabbed his hat, and his walking cane. He picked up a black bag – maybe a medical bag – I wasn't sure and left. Going to offer his medical expertise? I didn't know. I wasn't even sure if he was even still licensed to practice.

"Don't worry about locking up if you leave," Mac said opening the door. "I won't be gone too long."

After the whirlwind of Mac leaving died down, I looked at Bay and Micah. They were staring hungrily at the tray of cake. I took the glasses of milk and handed one to each of them, then picked up the tray.

"I brought these for Mac," I said. "And he's going to get them. Drink your milk, then bring me your glasses so I can rinse them out. I'm going into the kitchen, rewrap this cake, and put it up for him. Then we're leaving."

"Man, I don't know what you've gotten yourself into," Micah said to Bay. "She is so bossy."

"Don't I know it," Bay said shaking his head in mock exasperation. "Pray for me, Brother. Just please, pray for me."

On our walk home from Mac's, we crossed the greens and went past the town-square-slash-wedding-slash-crime-scene gazebo. I looked at Bay and sighed.

"Don't worry, Babe," he said. "It'll be okay."

"I don't know," Micah said. "The wedding is supposed to be day after tomorrow. You think the Sheriff'll pull that yellow crime tape down by then?"

"Now that they've found the hive-" Bay said.

"A hive that might be a clue," I interrupted.

"Now that they've found the hive," Bay repeated. "That tape might not come down as fast because Lloyd may think there's something more to find."

"They haven't dragged you into the investigation yet, huh?" Micah asked.

"They're trying," Bay said. "And if it was really an ancient artifact Kimmie brought back, then that's FBI territory."

Micah chuckled. "Arts and Culture Division."

"Yep. But we don't have different divisions in our small office. So our office is *every* division. And with me being from Yasamee, there's no doubt I'll be assigned to the case."

"You should have taken vacation days," I said.

"I was saving them in case we did Fiji," Bay said.

"I know," I said feeling bad for saying it in the first place. "And hopefully the Sheriff won't find anything amiss that could potentially bring you in," I said.

I didn't want to say that we hadn't found anything the night before.

1

"You told Mom there was a dig in Fiji," Micah said.

"There is, but Mom used to take Dad with her on digs. And us. I could take Bay."

We crossed over to Piedmont and headed to the B & B.

"I'm just hoping all the work that falls on me won't be too much for my new bride," Bay said. "And make it so I can't travel with her sometimes. I don't want her missing me too much."

"I don't think you have to worry," Micah said. "She was trying to pick up guys at the mall yesterday. I think she's got a plan on how to keep busy."

"I was not trying to pick up anyone," I said.

"I'd be careful, Bay," Micah continued, "Your grandmother might just be right. She said Logan's a little fickle."

I punched him.

Bay laugh. "Seems kind of cliché picking up guys at the mall, don't you think?" He put his arm around me.

"I was not trying to pick up anyone." I pulled away from Bay. "And I don't think he was trying to pick me up. He said I had something that belonged to him. Well, to 'us,' he said but he was all by himself." I remembered the confrontation. "He was acting pretty crazy you ask me."

"Wait. What?" Micah said. "You didn't tell me that. You just asked me had I seen him. Was he harassing you?"

I opened my mouth to talk then shut it. I didn't want to worry them by giving the wrong impression of what happened. "I really don't know how to describe it," I said. "He did kind of startle me. At first. Staring at me with those narrow, beady eyes." I thought about the encounter. "But I didn't feel like he was going to *hurt* me."

Both Micah and Bay stopped walking, but by the time I noticed I was a few steps ahead of them. I turned to face them. "C'mon. What are you two doing?"

"What exactly did that guy say to you?" Bay asked.

"I don't know. I think he said, 'You have something that belongs to us.'"

"What?" Micah said. "Who was he?"

"What do you have of his?" Bay asked.

"I don't know who he is," I said and then looked at Bay. "And I know I don't *have* anything of his."

"Are you sure that's what he said?" Bay asked.

"I said I don't know. I think that's what he said." I cocked my head to one side. "He could have said 'Would you like a buttercup?'"

"A buttercup?" Micah said and busted out laughing.

"Or, 'For some it's better not to fuss," I said and started laughing, too.

Bay didn't crack a smile. "This is not funny," he said. "You and my grandmother have been out here trying to solve murders, questioning folks, *accusing*

1

folks," he emphasized the word. "Like you're the police. Someone could be upset about it." He walked up to me and grabbed both my arms. "You have to take this seriously."

"Okay," I said and looked over at Micah. "I will." I lowered my eyes and tried to recall the incident. "He was an Asian guy. Never seen him before," I said. "I was getting my phone, putting away my ID and he walked up behind me and said something." I lifted my head to meet Bay's eyes. "When he saw Micah coming back, he left. That's all."

"He knew Micah?" Bay said and looked at my brother.

We both hunched our shoulders. "I don't think so," I said. "And Micah didn't see him, I know because I asked him if he had." I thought about it for a moment. "But you know, it was like he knew who Micah was because he left when he spotted him."

"Just like she said, I didn't see him," Micah said. I turned around and we started walking again. Me still ahead of them. "But, as far as I know." Micah continued after a moment's pause. "I don't know him, and I haven't seen anyone I know since I've been here."

"Have you seen anything strange lately?" Bay asked the both of us.

"You mean besides people getting murdered all the time?" Micah asked.

"You haven't even been here to see that," I said.

"I know what you've told me, Sis, and it's all very strange."

"Have you?" Bay asked us again.

"No. I haven't," Micah said.

"I saw a black car with tinted windows," I said and turned back to face them, walking backwards again. "Matter-of-fact, I saw the same car twice within a few minutes circling the town square around the time I found Kimmie's body."

"You can't circle a square," Micah said. "And a black car with tinted windows isn't strange."

"In Yasamee it is," Bay said. "Have you seen it since?"

"Nope," I said and shook my head. I turned around to face forward and stopped. I couldn't believe my eyes. I twisted my neck back around to Bay and Micah. "Until now."

1

Chapter Nineteen

The car was parked in the driveway of the
Maypop. And according to the boys, it was a 2016
BMW 750i with a V-8 engine, TwinPower Turbo
technology, 20" wheels, and had Illinois plates.

I'd seen the car now a few times, and I couldn't
have told them any of that. All I could add to the
conversation was what I had already said – it was
black with tinted windows.

Bay and I walked up the front steps with
anticipation. We were going to find out who'd been
trolling the streets of Yasamee hidden behind
darkened windows. Micah, other than thinking it was
a cool car, still didn't see anything to make a fuss
about. That's what living in a big city like Cleveland
would get you.

Bay stepped through the door first, holding it open
for me and Micah. I walked into the Maypop and
stopped dead in my tracks. Standing at the reservation
desk was the Asian guy from the mall that had spoken
to me. He turned, just as we walked through the door,

and when he saw me, a sly smile spread across his face.

Dressed in an Eisenhower cut black leather jacket, with straps and buckle accents on either side, he had on a pair of blue jeans and a black, mock turtleneck sweater. He stood next to another guy who, even from behind, was dressed like he worked on Wall Street.

I hit Micah, who was standing next to me. "That's him," I said pointing toward him with a nod of my head.

"Who?" he whispered back.

"The guy from the mall," I said. "The one that said I had something of his. Well his and someone else's." I looked at the other guy. "Maybe that's the 'someone else.'"

"Which one said something to you?"

"The one in the black leather jacket."

That answer made Micah step forward. "Yo," he said and tilting his head back, he jutted his chin out.

I shook my head. *He's been watching too many gangster movies*, I thought.

Both men turned around, and for the first time I saw Wall Street Guy's face. He was handsome, dimple in his chin, jet black hair neatly combed away from his face – nothing like his bad boy counterpart.

"May I help you?" Wall Street Guy asked.

"I'm talking to your friend," Micah said. "He had a problem with my sister at the mall the other day."

That statement made Bay step forward.

1

"Is this the guy from the mall, Logan?" he asked. "The one you just told us about?"

*Didn't he just hear Micah say it was?*

It was too much "tough guy-*ish*" stuff going on for me. I stepped forward.

"What did you say to me yesterday?" I asked thinking I could defend myself.

Wall Street Guy turned and looked at his friend and back at me. With a warm (probably fake) smile that showed a mouthful full of evenly aligned, brilliantly white teeth, he stuck out his hand. "Hello, I'm Nick Stavish, and this is my associate, Ho Yung."

No one stepped forward to shake his hand. Renmar, who'd apparently been checking them in, stood behind the counter with her mouth opened.

Nick Stavish pulled his hand back and chuckled. He looked at me, wiping the palms of his hands together. "I think perhaps you're mistaken." He looked at Ho, then back to me. "He didn't say anything to you."

"Yes, he did," I said. "He said that I had something that belongs to him."

"Do you know her, Ho," he asked his friend.

"No," Ho Yung said in that same acerbic tone. "Never seen her before."

"You've been driving around town," Bay said. "Evidently following her as well. What is your business in Yasamee?"

"We've just been chillin'," Nick said, the half-smile, half-smirk never leaving his face. "Minding our own business. Who wants to know?"

"I'm her fiancé, and part owner of this bed and breakfast. And if she says that your 'associate' spoke to her, I believe her." Bay looked at Renmar. "Were they checking in, Ma?" he asked.

She looked down at the register and back up at Bay. "They were," she said.

"Well, not anymore," Bay said. He looked at the two of them. "You'll have to find somewhere else to stay."

Nick Stavish swung from his waist and looked back at Renmar, then turned back locking eyes with Bay. "Ma'am, can you suggest another place in town for us." Speaking to Renmar, he never took his eyes off of Bay.

"No she can't," Bay said, narrowing his eyes at Nick. "And I suggest you leave. You and your friend. Now."

Nick Stavish looked around at all of us, blew out a breath, made a loud clap with his hands, and rubbed them together again. "Looks like we won't get a room here, Ho," he said. "We'll find another place to stay, and after that we can finish our business."

"As long as your 'business' doesn't have anything to do with her," Bay pointed his thumb my way. "You're free to do whatever you like. As long as it's legal."

1

"Oh are you threatening to sic your Sheriff on us? Doesn't he have his hands full right now?"

"What do you know about that?" I asked. "What the Sheriff is doing?"

Before he could answer, Bay placed his hand on my arm. "They're leaving. They don't have time for questions."

Bay opened the front door and stood waiting for them to go.

The two left without saying a word, but their faces spoke volumes. Bay and his "goon" Micah had seemingly started a turf war about something we knew nothing about.

"So what was that, Bay?" Renmar asked. "You running customers away?"

"I didn't like that guy."

"I didn't either," Micah said. "Neither one of them. Acting like the Green Hornet and Kato."

Bay started laughing. "Yeah, Man. They did, didn't they? That's so funny. Green Hornet. But his Kato didn't seem too tough to me."

"Why didn't you pull out your badge, Man?" Micah said still chuckling. "Show 'em you're the law."

"I don't need a badge to take care of my woman." Bay came and wrapped his arm around me tightly. "I'ma protect her 'cause I'm her man."

I rolled my eyes. "This isn't the Wild Wild West," I said. "You ran them away, and now we'll never know what they wanted."

"That Ho Yung wanted something from you," Bay said. "Evidently to give to Nick. Something that you don't have. I didn't want either one of them bothering you with their nonsense. Right now we've got a killer on the loose, probably someone from somewhere else, if they're importing hornets, and this guy's a stranger. They could have something to do with all of this."

"Yeah, Logan," Micah said. "Didn't Daddy teach you about stranger-danger?"

*Stranger Danger.* That just tickled the stew out of the two of them.

"Green Hornet and Kato?" my mother said to Micah. She chuckled. "How do you know about them? They came on TV when I was a little girl. Back in the 60s."

We were all sitting in the dining room, and I was telling my mother and Miss Vivee about our little run-in with our would-be guests.

"Reruns on Me-TV, Ma," Micah said. "And some of the episodes are on YouTube. Plus, they made a movie about it not too long ago."

"So what did those two want from you, Logan?" Miss Vivee asked. She scooted her chair up close to my mother's. She had really taken a liking to her.

"I don't know," I said. "And I'll probably never find out now that Micah and Bay, the two Yasamee *American Gangsters,* have run them away."

1

Micah made a face like he didn't know what I was talking about, and he would have been all alone in mounting any kind of a defense. Bay had left to go and speak to the Sheriff about the Beamer and its occupants.

"So why would they think that you had something of theirs?" my mother asked.

"At first, I didn't know, and I hadn't given anymore thought to it after I saw him in the mall. But then after I found he was associated with that car, I remembered something. The only thing I can think of is when I first found Kimmie. I was standing over her and I dropped something out of my pocket, and then I stooped down to pick it up."

"Did you see the car then?" Micah asked.

"I dunno. But he must have passed by then. I mean, I saw the car a couple of times that morning." I shrugged. "They must've seen me."

"So you think, that they think, that you took something off of that dead girl?" Micah asked.

I hunched my shoulders. "I don't know, but I'm thinking that had to be it."

"Why you think that?" Micah said.

"Because that's what he said. That Ho guy. He said, 'I saw you pick it up. Right next to that girl, you know the dead girl.' Or something like that." I did a not-so-good imitation of his voice.

"You didn't tell me that part," Micah said and frowned. "Did you tell Bay?"

"You heard what I told Bay, Micah."

"He thinks that you got something off the dead girl, and then he saw you at the mall and asked you about it?" my mother asked.

"Bay and I think he *followed* her to the mall," Micah said. "Because he knew who I was and I hadn't seen him. He must've seen us both get out the car."

"That's not good," my mother said.

"No. Not good." Miss Vivee nodded in agreement. "But maybe it was about the artifact that they found at Stallings Inn," Miss Vivee said. "Maybe they came looking for it. I'll have to add them to my suspect list."

"An artifact?" I looked at my mother. "They found an artifact?"

"The Sheriff found one when they did the search this morning," Miss Vivee said.

"So there really might be Artifact Hunters?" I said. "They were in the house last night? The same time we were?"

"The Sheriff couldn't tell who had been in the house," my mother said. "Or when. Thank goodness for that, or we might have to answer for it. And he said it wasn't as much of a mess as Frankie claimed."

"Good," I said because I didn't want to take the rest of my day cleaning up that place.

"They had your mother look at what they found." Miss Vivee smiled at my mother. "You should have seen her. Turning it over. Putting on gloves examining it. I was so proud of her."

1

*Proud? That's like been her job for thirty years. Especially in her position as curator of the Museum of Antiquity.*

I looked at my mother. She was the only one I was going to get a straight story from. One not filled with hyperbole. "Ma! Kimmie really did have an artifact from India?"

"Yeah, she did," my mother said.

"Wow," I said. "I wouldn't have ever thought that she would have something like that. Was it actually from the Bardaisan period?"

"It wasn't real," my mother said.

"What?" I said. "A fake relic? Oh my goodness. Really? Why would she do that?" I shook my head. "So, wait. Was someone after her for a fake artifact?"

"I don't know," my mother said.

"And," Miss Vivee raised an eyebrow. "It wasn't there last night."

I tilted my head and thought about that. "Well . . ." I started. "We really didn't get a chance to search much. Maybe we just missed it."

"They found it in her duffle bag," my mother said.

"The one we looked in?" I asked.

"Yes," she said. "At least it looked like the same one in the pictures the Sheriff showed me."

"Who put it there?" I asked.

"Probably the same person that "ransacked" the house," Miss Vivee said. "So, the real question is *why*?"

.

Chapter Twenty

It was getting late, dusk was settling in, and the crickets lulled us into an easy kind of mood. We were sitting on the front porch, my mother and Miss Vivee in the flower covered glider, and me in the large white rocker.

We were sipping iced tea and chatting, taking a rest from all the talk of murder. But that didn't stop us from talking about the other taxing topic that was looming over us. The wedding.

The investigation was at a standstill, at least on our end, and I was getting nervous about not being able to have it at the gazebo. Miss Vivee on the other hand, didn't seem worried at all. She was confident that all would go as planned. The murder wouldn't postpone the wedding or the venue. She was sure we'd have everything solved before Sunday's ceremony.

*I just wish I had her confidence.*

"Has Marge even been working on it?" my mother asked. "I would think she'd go with her contingency plan by now. Maybe I could speak with her?"

1

"I don't understand the idea of a wedding planner," Miss Vivee said. "You put out a couple of flowers, a few chairs for family, if'n they come, and grab a preacher. *Wham! Bam!* You're married."

"Very romantic," I said.

"I'm sure your mother will tell you, there is nothing romantic about being married," Miss Vivee said.

"In the beginning, there certainly is," my mother said and patted my hand. "Let's not fill Logan with discouragement, Miss Vivee. Not when she's so looking forward to hers."

"How about we go take a looksee at that gazebo," Miss Vivee said. "That'll make you feel better?"

"I'm not feeling bad, just a little anxious. I just want everything to go like we planned it."

"So it's settled," Miss Vivee said seemingly not understanding me. "We'll take a little drive. Check on the gazebo."

"That's not what I said."

"Get the car," she said. "Justin and I will wait for you here."

"Oh brother," I said, and drug myself out of the rocker. "I'll be right back."

"Will it be the wedding day before I meet Mac?" my mother asked. She and I were sitting on the steps of the gazebo. Miss Vivee was poking around in the flowers she'd had planted for the ceremony. She had me shine a light from one of the flashlights I'd bought for our burglary over her while she worked.

"Oh!" I said remembering. "When we went to see Mac, he had a magazine article about how honeybees kill hornets."

"What?" Miss Vivee said. She stopped fiddling with the plants and came over to me.

"Hornets are natural predators of honeybees," I said. And as a defense mechanism, they can generate enough heat to kill them."

"You saw that at Mac's house?" Miss Vivee asked.

"Yeah. When we went over. He had the magazine opened to that page. One of his National Geographic magazines."

"There were bees at the crime scene," Miss Vivee said.

"I remember," my mother said. "My big 'ole son was afraid of them."

"Mac must have used the bees to get rid of the evidence," Miss Vivee said.

"What?" my mother and I said almost in unison.

"That's why they couldn't find the hornet," Miss Vivee said.

"No one said they couldn't find the hornet," I said

"No one said they did find it, either," Miss Vivee said. "And did you tell me that Mac didn't have that mangy dog of his with him?"

"Rover is not mangy."

1

"He's a coonhound," Miss Vivee said. "That's about as mangy as you can get."

"Dog breed aside," I said. "You don't have anything to pin on Mac for that murder."

"Why else would Mac be out that early in the morning? Especially if he didn't have his dog. He should have known better," Miss Vivee said. "Rover could have given him an alibi."

"Mac didn't kill that girl," I said, this time with a little more force. "Hornets, I've learned, are not like bees, they don't die after stinging someone. It could have just flown off. And he was waiting for the florist to open. That's his alibi, not that he needs one."

"Likely story," Miss Vivee said.

"Mac couldn't do that," I said.

"If he didn't kill her then why did he get rid of the evidence?" she asked.

"Who said he got rid of the evidence?" I said, frustration surely evident in my voice.

"You did," she said.

"Oh. My. Gosh."

"I'm moving Mac up on my list," Miss Vivee said. "He has just become Suspect #1."

"You've only got three people on your list," I said.

"Not true," Miss Vivee said. "Justin and I added Nick Stavish and Ho Yung to my list. We decided to add them after the Sheriff found that relic."

"Fake relic," my mother added. "Which they probably didn't know."

I turned and looked at my mother. I knew it was hard not to be swept up into Miss Vivee's antics, but I'd thought my mother would have more restraint. She should have been setting an example for me.

"Look-a-there. Speak of the devil." Miss Vivee pointed across the street. "Isn't that the car that's been following you around?" Miss Vivee asked me, cutting our current conversation short.

"It wasn't following me," I said and watched it as it turned a corner. "I just saw it a couple of times."

"Well it's the one that your stalker was in."

"He wasn't a stalker-" I started to say, but then I realized I wasn't so sure that he wasn't.

"They're looking for that artifact," my mother said.

"They've already killed Kimmie for it," Miss Vivee said like the pairs' reason for being in Yasamee had been confirmed.

I clicked my tongue. "I thought you said September and Keith killed her," I said to Miss Vivee. "And you don't know, Ma, if they were looking for it or not."

"Maybe what they came looking for is in that car," Miss Vivee said.

"Why would they get what they want, put it in the car, and drive around town with it?" I asked.

"Maybe they were tired," Miss Vivee offered. "Didn't feel like driving back to wherever they came from this late."

I sucked in a breath and blew it out.

1

"Look," Miss Vivee said and pointed. "Isn't that them going into Jellybean's?" She looked at me. "The Green Hornet and Kato." She used Micah's analogy. "I wonder what they're doing."

"Probably going to eat," I said. "Why do you wanna know?"

"Just wondering," Miss Vivee said her voice trailing off.

"We're not going in Jellybean's and question them, Miss Vivee. If that's what you're thinking," I said. "They may be dangerous."

"Oh hogwash," she said and dismissed my words with a wave of her hand. "They haven't done anything to anyone. Maybe riffled through Frankie's things at Stallings Inn, but heck we did that. It's like that Nick one said, they've just 'been chillin.'"

"We're not going to Jellybean's," I said again.

"Well how about you drive me past it?" she asked. "Just so I can see in the windows."

"We can go that way when we go home," I said. "But that's it, Miss Vivee."

"Whew! You are so bossy," Miss Vivee said.

"I am not," I said and remembered when Micah had said I was to Bay. I didn't want to be like that. Bay would divorce me the first year we were married.

"Okay, Miss Vivee," I said, trying to sound less dictatorial. "I'll drive you past it."

And that was probably the reason I agreed to let her get out of the car and inspect that black car with the tinted windows with one of our flashlights. I didn't want to seem authoritative.

"Pull over," she had told me after we passed Jellybean's and saw the two of them just being served. I had gone around the same corner they had, my car now idling next to theirs. "I want to take a looksee."

"You are not getting out of this car," I should have said, whether it was domineering or not, but instead I said, "Be careful, Miss Vivee."

*I'm such a wimp.*

After I parked, she got out and circled the car shining the light on it. It was parked on a tree-lined street, the occupants of the neat row of houses apparently settled in for the night. She stood on the tree lawn in front of it and stared at it. "We need to search that car." Miss Vivee said and started kicking her toe around in the dirt, apparently looking for something.

"It's locked," I said. I went and stood by it, looking at it, then turned and looked back at her. "And I don't know how to break into it."

Miss Vivee walked up the driveway of the house where the car was parked.

"What are you doing?" I said in a whisper.

She let out a grunt, bent over and picked up what she had found.

"Watch yourself, Missy," she shouted and hurled an object my way.

1

I ducked as something flew by me, just missing my ear. It smashed into the car window, shattering it into pieces.

"Oh my gaaaawd!" I said in a strained whisper right before I ran to the next yard, did a side roll and landed behind a bush. Even my mother, her jiggling chest nearly smacking her in her face, tried to run and – I'm not sure if she planned it, or if she fell – hit the ground and rolled – well I guess you could call it a roll – under a bush.

Miss Vivee stood there. Not moving as if she was waiting to see what happened. Then in a split second it seemed, she was at the car shining the flashlight inside of it.

"There's nothing there," she said as if she really had expected to find a two-thousand-year old stolen artifact just laying right there on the car seat.

## Chapter Twenty-One

"I can't believe you threw a rock at that car window," I said. We'd made it back to the Maypop without any blazing sirens in pursuit, and were sitting at the kitchen table, except for my mom who'd gone to bed. I guessed she'd had enough for one day. Micah had wandered down when he'd heard us come in. He was eating cake and drinking a glass of milk.

"I can't believe that she was able to break the glass," Micah said. "That takes a little *umph*."

"I used to play baseball, Miss Vivee said.

"No you didn't," I said.

"I was the star pitcher."

I shook my head and looked at Micah. "No she wasn't."

"You remember that movie with that guy in it that coached a group of women baseball players during World War two? 'There's no crying in baseball.'"

"A League of Their Own," Micah said forking a big chunk of chocolate cake into his mouth.

"Yep," she said nodding. "That was about me."

I rolled my eyes.

1

"They had to change the names in the movie, you know, to protect the innocent," she said.

"Why would women baseball players from fifty-sixty years ago need protecting?" I asked.

"You'd be surprised," Miss Vivee said matter-of-factly.

"They had the real women at the end of the movie, you know," Micah said. "They showed their faces."

"I know," she said swinging her arm in abbreviated circles like she was warming up for the pitch. "I sent a stand-in. I can't afford for just anyone to see my face."

"Probably because she has warrants out for things like vandalism," I said.

Miss Vivee raised her eyebrows a la Groucho Marx.

I shook my head. "Don't believe her, Micah," I said. "According to her, she's over a hundred, used to be a stripper, is so adept in yoga that she can stretch her body twice its length, and now she used to play professional baseball."

"Know one thing for sure, Missy," Miss Vivee pointed a boney finger at me. "I do know Voodoo. So if you want to keep your head the size it is, you shouldn't mess with me."

Miss Vivee had gone to bed in a huff. I did feel bad for outing her, as it were, but I just couldn't help myself. She was going to land me in jail if she kept up with her antics, or in the morgue.

I stepped out of my jeans and pulled on my green and brown plaid pajama bottoms. I lifted my shirt over my head and snapped my bra off, throwing them into the hamper.

I had wanted to tell her that the only places where there were documented shrunken heads were in Ecuador and Peru, done by the Jivaroan tribes. And I knew she hadn't gone there and learned any Voodoo.

Jivaroan tribes . . .

I smiled. I still knew my stuff. I came up with that off the top of my head.

Buttoning up my pajama top, I thought, *maybe I will teach.* I've got a lot of knowledge stored up. I hopped onto the bed and propped my head on a pillow. I had forgotten that I was smart, too. Hanging around Mac and Miss Vivee with their vast knowledge had made me feel like I did when I was around my mother. Inadequate.

I turned on my back, lying across the bed, I stared up at the ceiling. There were a lot of colleges in Georgia. Especially up in Atlanta where Bay and I planned to live. Maybe even work in the Georgia Crime Lab as a forensic anthropologist . . .

*Yep, I could do that.*

Maybe that was my destiny in solving crimes. Not the one Miss Vivee wanted to encumber me with – following behind her as she went on her scatterbrained investigations, making up all of her tall

1

tales. But using a scholarly approach to finding out "whodunit" – maybe even working hand in hand with Bay like they do on that TV show *Bones*.

I fell asleep with a smile. I dreamt about me emerging from a grayish mist made by a bee smoker, with Bay guiding a handcuffed man into a squad car, and bees carrying the bones of our victim to its heavenly home. Birds were chirping, and the sun was shining . . .

Chapter Twenty-Two
Saturday, 8:30am

*One day before the wedding . . .*

The next morning, there was a tang coming from the kitchen, but it wasn't the delightful aroma of anything Renmar would cook.

Then I found out why.

Frankie was buzzing around the kitchen, humming a little tune, hand oven mitt covered, she was peeking through the top door of the double oven.

"What you doing?" I asked and took a seat at the big farm table. I'd brought my laptop down, I wanted to look up Kimmie's fake artifact.

"Fixing breakfast for everyone," she said. "What does it look like I'm doing?"

*I wasn't sure, because it didn't smell like anything I wanted to eat.*

"Where's Renmar?" I asked.

"Last minute wedding details," she said.

Miss Vivee and my mother wandered in through the back door.

1

"Morning," my mother said and smiled at me.

"Did you guys sleep in the greenhouse?" I asked.

"Of course not," my mother said. "We were checking on the flowers." She held up a collection of them. "We picked some for the tables in the dining room."

"Good morning," Micah said. He stood in the archway that led from the front of the house scratching his head. "Where's Renmar?" he said. "Isn't she cooking breakfast?"

"I'm cooking breakfast," Frankie said. "How do you like your eggs?" She dipped her head into the fridge and came out with a carton of them.

"Cooked by Renmar," Micah sat down and whispered in my ear.

I laughed and Frankie looked over at us. "What's funny," she asked and kicked the refrigerator shut.

"Nothing," we said together.

She looked at us out the corner of her eye before reaching up into the cabinet for a mixing bowl.

"Sit down, Justin," Miss Vivee said. "I'll make you some tea."

My mother came and sat on the other side of me, laying the flowers on the table. I lifted the lid on my laptop and powered it up.

"What are you doing?" she asked.

"Researching that *fake-o*," I said and looked at her.

"Ohhh," she said nodding. "I got you."

It wasn't that I was trying to keep it secret from anyone else in the room. But I'd learned over the past few days that Frankie always got so emotional about things. And if we had discovered that her stepdaughter was killed over a counterfeit relic, I'd hate to have to witness her eruption after learning the truth.

Micah hopped up and went to the cabinet and grabbed a glass. "Aargghh!" he squawked, out of the blue. "It's a bee!" He jumped away from it and tucked himself into a corner.

"How did that get in here?" my mother said, she stood up, apparently readying herself for battle with it.

"Probably from the garden," Miss Vivee said. "Maybe even in the flowers we brought in. We get them often. There's a swatter hanging on the wall by the door."

"Don't be silly," Frankie said. Still humming her little ditty, she grabbed a Mason jar out of the cabinet, poured a drop of honey in it, laid a tea towel over her shoulder, and then plucked a flower from my mother's bunch, putting it on top of the honey. She hovered the opened jar over the bee as it flittered around the bundle of flowers on the table, slowly swaying the jar back and forth, like she was using it to lull the bee into a trance. Then, as if she knew exactly the right time, she took the towel from her shoulder and laid it over the arm that held the jar, apparently to protect it from a potential bee sting. Then she swooped the bee into the jar, securely twisting the lid down.

1

Clapping ensued.

"Bravo!" I heard from the doorway and saw Brie and Renmar standing there, patting their hands together.

"I must say, Frankie," Renmar said. "I wouldn't mind you in my kitchen anytime if it meant no more bees."

"It was nothing," she said beaming. She walked over to the door, holding the screen open with her hip, she unscrewed the top and set the bee free.

"You can come out the corner, scaredy-cat," my mother said to Micah, chuckling.

"I'm not scared of that bee," he said. "I'm just afraid of getting stung. I'm allergic."

"Since when?" my mother said.

"You should have left it in the jar," Micah said.

"Noooo," Frankie said. "It would have gotten too hot, fluttering around in there. And how would it breathe?"

"All I care about is it stinging me," Micah said.

My mother shook her head "C'mon boy, sit over here by your mommy. I'll protect you."

I watched everyone as they celebrated Frankie ridding the kitchen of the bee. I thought about how she'd come and taken over the Maypop, upsetting the household, even putting Renmar out of her kitchen, more than likely hiding her grief in keeping busy with us, and now how everyone was happy she was here. I thought about how strong she'd been through it all. Kimmie dying. Her husband sick, with not too much longer to live, either. She'd be all by herself soon. And then I thought about her house being ransacked, how she had to put her household on pause – no income from the inn, bills piling up . . .

Then I thought about the mail at her house.

And the bee smoker from my dream.

I abandoned my search on the fake artifact and started a new Google search.

"Frankie," I said looking up from my computer after finding what I was looking for. "What does apiary mean?"

"Why would you'd think I'd know that?" she said, my question pulling her away from the accolades.

"It a place where beehives are kept," Miss Vivee said. "Why you ask?"

"Is it now?" I said and smiled. "Beehives."

"The mail," Miss Vivee said slowly, seemingly understanding, but she was cut-off by Bay before she could say anything else.

"Morning all," Bay said as he strode into the room.

I turned and looked at him, a smirk on my face.

"Happy to see me?" he said and bent over and plopped a kiss on my lips. "'Cause you're looking a little strange."

I turned and looked at my mother and then Miss Vivee. A grin spreading across my lips. "Not feeling strange," I said shaking my head. "Just enlightened."

"Enlightened?" Bay asked.

1

"Hmmm-mmm." I nodded. "I just figured out who killed Kimmie Hunt."

Chapter Twenty-Three

"Yesss," I said, almost in a whisper. "I've figured it out."

I was tingling all over, my heart was racing, and I had to make a conscience effort to slow down my breathing.

*Is this what Miss Vivee felt like when she's figured it all out?*

What a rush.

"You did?" my mother said, her face gleaming. "You figured it out?" She pushed my arm, jarring me away from my mental happy dance.

"You did not," Miss Vivee said.

"Yes, I did." I nodded slowly. "And you know, too, don't you?"

Miss Vivee winked at me.

"Well, are you going to tell us?" Micah asked. "Or are you just going to sit there grinning. I'm hungry and now it looks like I'll have to wait even longer to eat."

"It wasn't an accident," I said and pointed to Micah. "That hornet could have live long enough to

1

make the trip per its lifespan, but it would've been depleted of oxygen long before. It didn't stay hidden in Kimmie's suitcase. Frankie putting that bee in the jar made me think of that. Plus, why would Kimmie Hunt pack a nylon jogging suit, with long pants, and a long sleeved jacket on a trip where it's hot? Very hot, right Ma."

"Yes," my mother said. "That's what I remember from when I was there excavating."

"And remember," I said, "what Frankie said about that jogging suit?" I said.

"She said she made Kimmie put it on," Renmar said slowly as if the realization just hit her.

All heads turned to Frankie.

"What?" Frankie said and swallowed hard.

"You put that hornet in her jogging suit," I said.

"I did no such thing," Frankie said. "I wanted her to stay warm. She had a slight fever. I told you all that. And that's why I wanted her to put it on."

"You wanted her to work up a sweat," I said. "Because you knew that those hornets were drawn to sweat."

"And people running," Micah said, apparently remembering the article we'd read the first day he got to Yasamee.

"Don't be ridiculous," Frankie said. "How would I know that?"

"You know because you know all about bees," I said. "Don't you?"

"What?" she said.

"I saw an envelope in your mail from Gardner's Apiaries over in Baxley, Georgia. The front of it said 'Invoice Enclosed.'"

"I saw it, too," Miss Vivee said. "But until now I didn't give it a second thought."

She swallowed again. "I bought honey from them," she said her voice shaky. "I use it for my tea."

"Why don't you just buy it at the store?" Miss Vivee asked.

"They don't sell honey," I said. I turned my laptop around to show where I had their website pulled up. "It's for beekeepers. They sell queen bees and hives. Nothing else."

"Did you buy a beehive, Mrs. Hunt?" Bay asked Frankie, then looked at me. "Where is this place?"

"Baxley," Miss Vivee said. "The envelope gave an address over in Baxley. Down near Savannah." She looked at Frankie. "That's where Nash Hunt has been going to see the doctor. It's where all his medicine is from."

"Who told you that?" Frankie said. She backed up and leaned on the sink. "Have you two been snooping around in my house?"

"The three of us have," my mother said speaking up. "And we know that there wasn't any artifact, real or otherwise, in Kimmie's suitcase. At least not until you claimed it had been ransacked. Did you put that fake there?"

"No! Of course I didn't," Frankie said, her eyes were filling up with tears.

1

Abby L. Vandiver

"Bay," my mother said, not taking her eyes off of Frankie. "Perhaps you should check that little relic for fingerprints. Someone had to handle it to put it where the Sheriff found it."

"Wait," Brie said. "I'm still trying to figure out what bees have to do with hornets?"

I looked at Frankie, and Frankie looked at me.

"Hornets are natural predators of honeybees, aren't they Frankie?" I said. She didn't say a word. "And anyone that knows about bees would know that, wouldn't they?" I pointed with my head to the jar she'd caught the bee with, still sitting on the table.

"I let one little bee out of the house, and you accuse me of murder," Frankie said. "Bay," she said turning to him. "You're law enforcement. You know all of this is bogus, don't you?" She tried to smile, but her lips were trembling too much for it to stick.

"It wasn't Mac trying to get rid of evidence," I said and looked at Miss Vivee. "It was Frankie. She's the one that put that beehive out by the gazebo that Junior Appletree found. She knew it would kill the hornet."

"Bought it from that apiary in Baxley, and probably kept it in that shed she calls a greenhouse until she needed it."

"Why would I kill Kimmie?" Frankie said.

"Because just like you said, Frankie," Miss Vivee said. "Kimmie was gallivanting all over the world spending up Nash Hunt's money. You thought if she kept it up, there wouldn't be any left for you."

"He is still making money."

"He wouldn't be making any money after he died," Miss Vivee said. "And that's a real possibility seeing that he has lung cancer, isn't it?"

"You'd be broke," I said.

Frankie let out a nervous chuckle. "We would have gone broke long before then the way Kimmie was spending money."

"You said you were the one that killed Kimmie," Renmar said her eyebrows arched, her voice accusing. "You admitted to it."

"I didn't mean it," she said. "I was just . . ." She swiped her hand over her face. "Distraught."

"Or was it because you really were *guilty*," Miss Vivee said.

1

Epilogue
Sunday, 10:00am

*The wedding day . . .*

I'd never dreamed of having a wedding like most little girls do. Waiting for Prince Charming to come and sweep me off my feet, and we'd live happily ever after, just hadn't been my cup of tea. My idea of the "ever after" was being able to dig up ancient civilizations and letting them live again as I pieced together their history. And that certainly made me happy. And once I got engaged, I had decided that I didn't want much or a lot of fuss. But today, the day of the wedding, I was filled with butterflies and excitement. It was a magical feeling, and I finally understood why people spent thousands of dollars for the one day.

I stood in front of my chevel mirror. I placed the second magnolia flower into my upswept do. Turning from side to side, I smiled at what I saw.

"You look beautiful," my mother said.

I turned and saw her and my father standing in the doorway. He'd made it into Yasamee right as Bay was carting Frankie out in handcuffs.

"My little girl," my father said. "All grown up."

"I'll never be too grown-up to be your little girl, Daddy," I said.

"Yoohoo!" we heard drifting down the hallway. "Yoohoo!" yelled again.

"But we can't forget about Miss Vivee," I said just as she came to my room. My parents parted and she floated in."

"Oh, Miss Vivee you look -"

"Lovely." She finished my sentence.

"I was going to say 'beautiful,'" I said.

"Yes, but I've always loved that word. Lovely. I want to be called that."

"You are lovely, indeed," my father said and took her hand and kissed it. "Absolutely lovely."

Miss Vivee blushed and it seemed I saw a tear come to her eye. "Has anyone seen Mac?" Miss Vivee asked and sniffed to keep from letting it fall.

"He wouldn't be here!" my mother said and chuckled.

"Mother," Renmar yelled from downstairs.

"They sure do yell a lot around here," my father said.

"Not usually," I said.

"Mother," Renmar yelled again. This time she sounded closer, her footsteps giving away how near she was. "Are we just going to mill around?" She'd

1

come into my room and surveyed us all gathered there. "You can't get married with the clock going toward the hour if you're not there when it strikes have past." She clapped her hands to disperse us. "Let's go! We have a wedding to get to!"

As we rode in the open carriage, drawn by two white horses to the town square, I thought about the last three days. Miss Vivee had been right, the murder had been solved and the wedding was taking place as scheduled. She hadn't wavered, nor had she ever showed an ounce of worry. It was as if she truly held firmly to the notion that love would conquer all.

I hope that all my life I will have that much faith in it. The faith that the love I give to others, and that they give to me will teach me hope and to believe without waver, give me strength, sustain me and carry me through all my days.

There's an old wives' tale that says that "If you kill a bee, you'll have bad luck." Frankie had spared one, and bad luck still rained down on her. Frankie's problem? She hadn't counted on love to see her through. The love Kimmie had given her in trusting, and accepting her to be her mother. Or the love that Frank showed, providing that even in the case of his death he would see to her well-being. Frankie had figured to make it in this life, she had to look out for herself, whatever it took. And in her estimation, it took killing Kimmie.

*Talk about a wicked stepmother . . .*

And come to find out, Frankie had had a hand in the practical joke Kimmie was playing on September. Maybe even being the one who thought it up, and planting the fake relic. It looked like Frankie had taken a lot of time and care to plan the murder, figuring out a way to hide the evidence, even raising "reasonable doubt" as Micah put it, by pointing the finger at the possibility that someone else killed Kimmie to get the artifact they thought she had.

We pulled up to the town square and it was filled with people. Bright colors, large hats, small potted trees adorning the yard with twinkling clear lights, and the smell of flowers filled the space. Wooden folding chairs with white slipcovers, tied down with gold sashes, were on either side of the center aisle that was covered with white rose petals. Off to the side, next to the string quartet was a Hammond tonewheel organ that Miss Vivee had had "Deputy" Junior Appletree wheel over from the Baptist church, and at the center was the gazebo.

It was beautifully decorated. More than I could have imagined. Whimsical and elegant – it was a happily-ever-after, storybook backdrop if I'd ever seen one. The underside of the roof had been draped in white tulle, intertwined with garlands of vines and soft pink flowers. Sprays of bright, deep pink and white flower arrangements were hung around it, and

1

at its entrance. It gave me a sense of ecstasy and happiness, and I seemed to swell with a blissfulness that every woman on her wedding day must feel.

I spotted Mac, looking dapper in his tuxedo, and tried to make my way over to him. But before I could go, I saw Marge coming toward me in a rush.

"What are you doing?" she said, her eyes wide. "We're getting ready to start! Get in place!"

So I took my place, and waited for the music to cue. But as I waited, I suddenly got so nervous that it felt as if I couldn't breathe. I felt my knees buckle and I was dizzy. I put my hand on the back of a chair to balance myself, and then I saw Miss Vivee. She was calm as a summer's breeze, looking – lovely – and I closed my eyes and took in a deep breath wanting to fill-up on the composure and serenity exuding from her.

I opened my eyes, and there stood my father. He smiled at me, and stuck out his arm. I took it and he walked me down the aisle. The butterflies flitting away with every step we took

Taking my place next to Mac at the altar, I whispered, "Where have you been?"

"I wanted to steer clear of Vivee," he said out of the side of his mouth.

"Why?" I whispered back, trying to hide the look of shock I knew was evident on my face.

"Because I didn't want to do anything to make her change her mind," he said through clenched teeth maintaining his wide smile.

"I don't think you have to worry about that," I said as the organ hit a chord, and the yard became still. I nodded down the aisle, and there was Miss Vivee, the loveliest bride I'd ever seen.

She made her first step, holding on to Bay's arm just as the organ and string quartet played the opening note of Wagner's *Bridal Chorus*. Dressed in a lace, Victorian style gown, she wore a crown of flowers. Miss Vivee seemed to glide over the flower petals strewn underfoot, her three foot train following. Bay's faced gleamed with pride, and as his eyes met mine, he winked.

Before they made it all the way down the aisle, Mac walked up to meet Miss Vivee and took her hand. He looked at Bay as if to say, "I've got her," then escorted her the rest of the way to the altar.

"Who gives this woman to be married to this man?" the preacher asked.

"I do," Bay said, then acting as the Man of Honor, took his place, coming to stand by me, Mac's Best Woman, and gently took my hand. "I love you," he leaned in and whispered. "And I can't wait until you are *my* bride."

## THE END

1

Thank you for taking time to read *Garden Gazebo Gallivant*. Look for more books in the Logan Dickerson Cozy Mystery Series coming soon. If you enjoyed it, please consider telling your friends about it. And don't forget to take the time to post a short review.

*http://amzn.to/2ejESTz*

# A Note from the Author

Were you surprised at whose wedding it was?
*Gotcha!*

Who would have ever thought Mac would wear Miss Vivee down? Well, other than Mac himself. I'm glad he did, us old people need love, too.

So, we're winding down the Logan Dickerson Cozy Mystery series, only one more to go – *South Seas Shenanigans*. Then I'll write a prequel, *A Lesson in Murder* that features Miss Vivee as a younger woman learning her craft in New Orleans. I expect to publish *South Seas Shenanigans* later this year, or early next year, and I'm not quite sure of the publication date for the prequel. I hope to start a new cozy mystery series soon. It will be a paranormal series.

But let me not get ahead of myself. In this series, as you know, Logan Dickerson is the daughter of the main character, Justin Dickerson, in my *Mars Origin "I" Series*. (So if you like mysteries with just a touch of sci-fi, you might want to check them out!). Like in *Incarnate*, in this book, Logan and her mom team up to solve the whodunit. (Way to include my old characters in my new book, huh?).

Justin, who is a Biblical archaeologist, and Micah, Logan's brother visit from Cleveland. Taking place again in the fictional town of Yasamee, in this installment we're all set for a wedding!

As always, I throw a little history in my books. This one is no different. The story of Bardaisan as told by Justin is true. Thomas started a church in India while John and Paul wrote parts of the canon, and the psalms in it are accredited to Bardaisan (bar-Daisan (son of Daisan) in Aramaic, which Justin speaks. That's the reason I used both spellings in the book). Bardaisan was born in Edessa and was a gnostic. He is credited with being a scientist, scholar, astrologer, philosopher and poet.

And as the first three book in this series, I am dedicating this book to a grandchild. This one is for September. She is the calm in the sea of rambunctiousness that are the Longino grandchildren. And hers is the only book where her dedication and name appear together.

And for all you brides, did you know having *something old* represents continuity; *something new* offers optimism for the future; *something borrowed* symbolizes borrowed happiness; and *something blue* stands for purity, love, and fidelity? It's a tradition that goes back a long way.

Thanks to my beta reader and friend, Kathryn Dionne. You never fail me, and as always, the book is better because of you.

I appreciate all my reviews and look forward to reading what you thought about my book. Grammatical errors are of course unintended, so if you find any, just email me and let me know what you've found.

I love connecting with my readers and look forward to chatting with you.

# Read My Other Books

Bed & Breakfast Bedlam
A Logan Dickerson Cozy Mystery
*http://amzn.to/1Ar6zkr*

Coastal Cottage Calamity
A Logan Dickerson Cozy Mystery
*http://amzn.to/1SvL1Z4*

Maya Mound Mayhem
A Logan Dickerson Cozy Mystery
*http://amzn.to/1fah16e*

Food Fair Frenzy
A Logan Dickerson Cozy Mystery
*http://amzn.to/2blGgne*

South Seas Shenanigans
A Logan Dickerson Cozy Mystery

In the Beginning
Mars Origin "I" Series Book I
*http://amzn.to/1cwDnd2*

Irrefutable Proof
Mars Origin "I" Series Book II
*http://amzn.to/1bwWjFt*
Incarnate
Mars Origin "I" Series Book III
*http://amzn.to/1y2Soy0*

At the End of the Line

*http://amzn.to/1fg7DYy*

**Coming Soon**

Deep Delta Devilry – a Logan Dickerson Cozy Mystery

A Lesson in Murder – A Logan Dickerson Cozy Mystery

Angel Angst – A Normal Junction Cozy Mystery

Witches Wheel – A Normal Junction Cozy Mystery

Ghostly Gadfly – A Normal Junction Cozy Mystery

Get a FREE eBook of my first novel, In the Beginning, when you sign up for my newsletter. I'll never spam you, I promise, you'll just get updates on my books. Visit my website at www.abbyvandiver.com to get your book

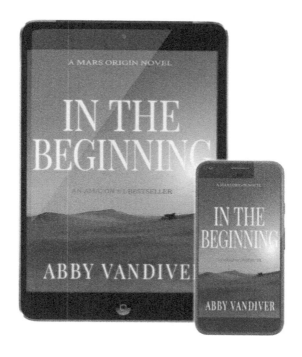

What if the history you learned in school wasn't the truth?
2,000 year old manuscripts. A reluctant archaeologists. A world changing discovery.
In the Beginning, an alternative history story.

Made in the USA
Monee, IL
29 December 2023